FECES OF

Harrison Phillips is an English author of extreme horror and splatterpunk fiction. His literary influences range from Clive Barker and Stephen King, to Jack Ketchum and Edward Lee. He was born and raised in Birmingham, England, where he still resides with his long-suffering wife, their two daughters, and a schnauzer named Minnie.

www.twitter.com/harrisonhorror

www.facebook.com/harrisonphillipshorror

vestigialpress@hotmail.com

Copyright © 2023 Vestigial Press

Cover artwork by
InsaneCamel
(insanecamelcorp@gmail.com)

Harrison Phillips has asserted his right to be identified as the author of this work.

All rights reserved. This book, or any portion thereof, may not be reproduced or used in any manner, without the express written permission of the publisher.

This book is a work of fiction. All names and characters are the product of the authors imagination. Any resemblance to actual persons, living or dead, is entirely coincidental.

FECES
OF
DEATH

The following story is based
on true events...

PROLOGUE
The Delivery

Dwight hated his job.

Let's be clear on that one, simple thing. He hated it. He didn't *dislike* it. He didn't consider it a *mild annoyance*. He *hated* it. He hated it more than anything else in the world, and there was little more to be said on the matter.

But it wasn't just the job itself that he hated. He hated the company that he worked for. He hated the *people* that he worked for. He hated the fact that *they* felt this job was only worth minimum wage. How was that even fair? Sure, there were plenty of other jobs out there that he could take - he'd been reminded of this fact about a dozen times in the last week alone - but none of them would pay him better, not with his meagre list of sub-par qualifications. *C grade in mathematics? Very fucking good. Congratulations.*

And yes, he *had* agreed to the terms of his contract, when he'd signed on that dotted line. But still, that didn't make it right, did it?

Dwight was a delivery driver for a large logistics company. They were probably turning over tens-of-millions each year, and here he was, damn-near living hand to fucking mouth. They had him driving the length and breadth of the country, sometimes behind the wheel for twelve hours straight, transporting goods from one multi-million-dollar corporation to another. That was the bread and butter of the company; without him, they were nothing. Yet they still managed to treat him like dog shit.

Fuck it.

The job itself wasn't *entirely* terrible; it wasn't as if he was *entirely* adverse to driving. It wasn't that part he hated. Sometimes, he actually enjoyed it, out on the open road, alone with his thoughts. No – what really made this job suck so fucking hard, was the fact that he had to work through the night.

That had never been part of the plan. Not that Dwight had ever really *had* a plan. But, most certainly he'd never intended to be a delivery driver. The truth was, he'd never *intended* to be *any* of the things he'd ended up being over the years.

He had, for a short while – back when he was still a teenager, fresh out of high school – hoped to become an engineer of some sorts, maybe even a motor mechanic. He'd even gone to college and everything. But he'd dropped out just halfway through the second term, having grown bored of all the know-it-all boffins trying to educate him. That was… What was it? Twenty years ago now? Maybe a little less – Dwight forgot his own age most of the time. However long ago that was, giving up so easily was something he now regretted, as doing so had led him to the string of thankless jobs he'd had since.

He'd flipped burgers at McDonalds. He'd washed cars at a local garage. He'd swept the floors of a beauty salon (that job hadn't been so bad, what with all the sexy, prick-teasing women who frequented the place - none of whom ever seemed to even acknowledge his existence). Probably the most interesting job he'd had was working in a factory, assembling electronic toys for children. He'd been fired from that job however, for forgetting to install the screws that secured the battery compartment one too many times. He could've *killed* a child, or so he was told.

Somewhat unnerving was the fact that this thought amused him no end.

Driving the flat-bed truck in which he was now sitting was the latest in that long line of bullshit menial jobs in which he'd found employment.

Tonight's bullshit assignment was carting a load of chemicals from PharmaCom's northern plant, to their sister site in the south of the country. Dwight wasn't any kind of a scientist – he'd be the first to hold his hands up on that count – so the truth was that he had no idea as to what the sixteen barrels he was currently transporting actually contained. What he *did* know however, was that there were various symbols on the side of each barrel, that meant whatever it was inside them was some real nasty shit.

!!!WARNING!!!
!!!TOXIC!!!
!!!BIOHAZARD!!!

Dwight was just grateful he didn't have to touch them; they'd been loaded by forklift at point A, and would be similarly *un*loaded at point B.

According to the SatNav, his destination was just a few miles up the road. Good. The weather was bad tonight; torrential rain battered the road, and made visibility poor, even as his windscreen wipers beat furiously back and forth. Thankfully, the roads on which he'd been driving had remained entirely empty (as was to be expected at three in the morning).

Dwight was tired, his eyes growing heavy; one of the many downfalls of driving during the night. He didn't mind admitting that there had been a few occasions when he had fallen asleep at the wheel – only for a split second, mind you – but long enough for him to shit his pants as soon as he realised what had happened. Praise be to God – not that he was a religious man at all – that he hadn't just ploughed head-on into oncoming traffic.

He was determined that this wasn't ever going to happen again; not after the last time, when he came precariously close to side-swiping an eighteen-wheeler. He knew who would've come off worse from *that* encounter. As such, he pulled a can of Red Bull from the glove compartment and popped it open, guzzling the whole thing back in one gulp. He crushed the can in his hand, then tossed it into the passenger-side footwell.

He then reached into the pocket of the jacket that had been screwed up on the passenger seat, and retrieved a packet of cigarettes. He pulled a cigarette from the pack and placed it between his lips.

Where the fuck was that goddamn lighter?

Screw it. The flat bed was old enough that it still had its own cigarette lighter. Most vehicles had done away with those now, but not Dwight's trusty old wagon. He pushed the lighter into its socket, until it clicked into place.

A few moments passed before the lighter popped back out, indicating that it was ready for use.

Dwight pulled the lighter out of the socket and used it to scorch the end of his cigarette, pulling in hard inhalations, until the tobacco finally caught alight. He cracked open the window, exhaled, then returned to lighter to its rightful place.

He returned his eyes to the road.

There was something there. A streak of black and white at first, then two glowing orbs, reflecting the headlights of the rapidly approaching vehicle.

Dwight slammed his foot down on the brake, as if he were trying to put his heel through the floor. But it was too late. The poor creature – a badger, as it so happened – squealed as it was dragged under the wheels of the truck, skin splitting, bones breaking, blood cascading down the windscreen, quickly washed away by the rain.

Steel screeched as Dwight tried to maintain control of the vehicle. Skidding along the road, slaloming from side to side, the water settling on the tarmac only serving to make the issue a hundred times worse than it already was, Dwight could only watch in the rear-view mirror, as the straps that had been used to tie the barrels into the bed of the truck came loose.

"Oh, fuck me!" Dwight muttered angrily to himself, as he watched the barrels tumble from the truck, bouncing away and rolling down the road. "No!"

As soon as the truck had finally stopped, then Dwight jumped out of the cab. The rain saturated his hair and his clothes immediately, soaking him through to the bone.

What a fucking mess.

Around half the barrels had fallen from the truck. Dwight hopped up into the bed and shoved those barrels which had remained back into place. He then used one of the straps to secure them, taking his time to ensure that they couldn't shift any further, no matter what.

Back down on the road, he began to roll the fallen barrels back towards the truck. Dwight wished he'd worn gloves; the steel of the barrels felt slick to the touch, but it was most likely just rainwater. It didn't seem like any of them had split.

"I'm so fuckin' fired," Dwight groaned to himself, as he worked to return the barrels to the truck. "I'm dead! They're gonna fuckin' *kill* me!"

The barrels were heavy. Dwight grunted as he lifted each one, the exertion making him feel as though he might just soil himself. It took him nearly fifteen minutes to return all the barrels to the bed of the truck. There was just one left, laid on its side, a few hundred yards along the road. Dwight jogged along the road and hopped over the barrel.

His feet squelched as they landed in something soft and malleable.

Dwight looked down to find himself standing in the spilled entrails of the badger he'd squashed just moments ago, his brand new Reebok classics now splattered with gore. *Pissed off* was an understatement. "Jesus *fuckin'* Christ," he said, kicking away the mangled intestines, all of a sudden realising that he now hated this job more than ever.

Feces Of Death

The carcass of the badger sat just a few feet away. Its body was almost entirely flat, the stomach split open, the viscera leaking out. Its skull had been crushed, mangled brain oozing out of a dismantled eye socket. Still, both eyes remained intact. And they were staring at him.

"What the fuck are you looking at?" Dwight muttered under his breath, his heart suddenly racing, the sight of the mutilated animal making him feel somewhat nauseous.

He rolled the last of the barrels back to the truck and hoisted it into the bed. He then used the straps to secure them in place, double-checking – then triple-checking – that they were all held firm.

Convinced that they could no longer move, he checked one last time, ensuring he hadn't missed any barrels. Happy that they were all accounted for, he jumped back into the cab of his truck, glad to finally be back out of the rain, and took off along the road, lighting himself another cigarette.

But Dwight had been incorrect; not *all* the barrels were accounted for. Fat use that C grade had been after all…

Unbeknownst to him, there were now only fifteen barrels in the back of his truck, not sixteen. One of the barrels had bounced through the trees, disappearing through the undergrowth, rolling away down a steep bank.

Worse was the fact that, as it had careened down the slope, it had crashed into a number of rocks, each of which had battered the steel, denting it inward, splitting it open, allowing the chemical inside to spill.

Worse still was the fact that, at the bottom of this slope, the barrel had landed in a stream, the heavy rain having caused the water to swell and the speed of the current to increase exponentially. The contents of the barrel ran into the water, dragged along the stream, through an overflow grate and into the sewers below.

Three weeks later…

CHAPTER ONE
Dog Shit Blues

Sandra loved that little dog of hers. She couldn't see it for the little shit that it really was.

His name was Toby. He was a mongrel of some kind; he had to be at least fifty percent Yorkshire terrier – God only knew what else he had in him. He had golden hair and ears too big for his head, and if anybody dared to get within twelve metres of him, he transformed into a demon, all gnashing teeth and high-pitched yaps.

Every day, Derek watched from the kitchen window of his bungalow, as Sandra would come shuffling along the path outside, barely lifting her feet, the arthritis having done a real number on her knees and ankles. She must've been around ninety; Derek often wondered just how many years she had left in her.

That was, without question, the worst thing about getting old; everybody started dying.

Derek was already eighty-two himself. He'd lost Wendy, his wife – God, how he missed her so – four years ago now. She'd only been seventy-five at the time. She should've had so many years left; they still had so many memories to make together. At least the cancer had taken her quick. Nobody had even known she had it, not until she'd collapsed and had to be rushed into hospital. She'd remained unconscious, and died just six hours later.

She hadn't suffered. Derek was thankful for this.

He lived alone now. After Wendy had died, the three-bedroom house they'd shared for the past forty-four years just felt too big. As such, he had decided to downsize. He sold the house and moved into the bungalow. It was a nice place, on a nice estate. Most of the residents there were people like him; widowers, not yet incapable of looking after themselves – not yet in need of being moved into a residential care home – but no longer quite so able to make those regular journeys up and down the stairs.

Derek didn't know much about Sandra. He *assumed* she was a widower, just like him, but he didn't know that for sure. Perhaps she'd always lived alone. She struck him as being a very quiet woman, very independent. A little antisocial, even.

Still, Derek would always offer a friendly wave as he saw her approaching, with Toby at the full extent of his retractable lead, Sandra doing little to prevent him wandering onto the other resident's lawns (not that there was much that she *could* do about it).

It was there that Toby would often do his business – seemingly on Derek's lawn, more often than not. If it were anybody else's dog, then Derek most certainly would've said something. But as it was Sandra, he had always kept his opinion on the matter to himself. He was sure that she *would have* cleaned up

Feces Of Death

the mess, if she were capable. But the fact remained that she *wasn't* capable; the way she dragged herself along the path – straight legged, her back stiff – told Derek everything he needed to know about her lack of mobility. Were she to bend down, he doubted she'd ever be able to straighten up again. Her picking up dog shit from the ground was pretty much out of the question.

Unless she was faking it, of course. But Derek very much doubted it.

And so, Derek had taken to picking up the crap from his own lawn, now purchasing a packet of poop scoop bags on his fortnightly visit to the supermarket.

Today, like usual, Toby scooted along to the middle of Derek's lawn, squatted on his haunches, arched his back and dropped a steaming turd right there on the grass. Sandra, like usual, offered a smile and a curt wave, to which Derek replied in kind. Then, Sandra and Toby were gone, waddling and scurrying away, respectively.

She could've at least apologised. She didn't need to look so pleased with herself.

Derek always liked to give it a minute before going out there to clean up the mess; he didn't want Sandra seeing him, and thinking him rude. Not that it *was* rude. It was rude of *her* to allow her dog to use his lawn as its own private bathroom. Still, *he* never said anything about *that*.

Regardless, he gave it a minute.

Outside, the sun was shining. It was a pleasant day, despite all the rain they'd been having recently. The air was warm, if not a little humid. With his slippers on, Derek crossed the lawn, placing his hand inside the poop scoop bag as he went, and located the turd. There, he crouched, picked up the poop (it was soft and squidgy and entirely unpleasant), folded the bag inside out, tied the handles into a knot, and dropped it into the outside bin.

Derek was about to return to his home when the shrill sound of screaming emanated from somewhere along the street.

At first, a thousand questions ran through Derek's mind - Who? What? How? Why? - none of which seemed to have any answer forthcoming. But then, as the screaming continued, he knew that any answer would be completely irrelevant. He just needed to do something.

Quickly, he sprinted across the lawn, curling his toes upwards to prevent his slippers from falling off his feet, and leaving him barefoot on the pavement. As he ran along the street, he found that his kneecaps were beginning to burn – an unfortunate side effect of growing old, no doubt. The thin, worn-out soles of his slippers offered little cushioning against his feet, as his heels pounded the pavement.

Thirty seconds later, and Derek turned the corner at the last bungalow in their row. Immediately, he saw to whom the scream had belonged.

It was Sandra.

She was standing over an open drain, the heavy, cast iron manhole cover somehow shifted to one side. The cord of the retractable lead trailed off, down into the darkness below.

That dumb dog must've fallen in!

Or perhaps not. Sandra was leaning back, her face strained, as if she were fighting with all her might to keep a grip of the plastic handle. The way she looked reminded Derek of all those times spent fishing in his youth, when he and his father would battle for supremacy over the trout below the surface of the lake, trying desperately to not let go of the rod.

He rushed over to her. "What's going on?" he demanded, as if it were *she* who was somehow doing something wrong. He received no answer of course; Sandra was too busy fighting to keep her poor little doggy from being dragged off into the depths of the underworld.

Derek could see that the lead was tight, pulled to its full extension, no slack remaining within the handle. Sandra rocked back and forth on her heels, as something tried to pull her in.

What the fuck was going on?

No time for such questions. Derek sprang into action. He circled behind Sandra and wrapped his arms around her waist, reaching forward to take a hold of the lead with one hand, his fingers curling around the plastic body, his other hand grasping her weak wrists. Together they held tight. Derek could feel the force of whatever it was on the other end of the lead, pulling with all its might. *Jesus!* It *was* like those fishing trips after all!

Suddenly, instantaneously, the force was severed, sending both Derek and Sandra sprawling backwards onto the tarmac. Both of Derek's elbows smashed painfully into the tarmac, the skin scraped away. But that was fine; he'd be okay – he was more concerned about Sandra, and the fact that she could've broken a hip. Thankfully, he'd cushioned her landing.

But Sandra didn't seem at all interested in her own wellbeing. She was entirely focused on the cord of the retractable lead, winding its way back into the handle.

Derek watched as the striped cord whipped its way out of the drain, dragging with it the filth of the sewers below. And then came the dog's collar.

But no dog.

No Toby.

Sandra held the collar up, her breathing racked by heavy sobs.

Derek couldn't believe his eyes. The collar had been torn to shreds. The material was frayed along the length, chunks torn from the sides, flaps of withered nylon hanging loose. Most distressing was the fact that it was saturated with blood. There even seemed to be a small sliver of flesh clinging to the sodden material, what remained of the dog's fur now stained crimson.

Tears streaked down Sandra's cheeks. "Oh my God!" she moaned. "OH MY GOD!"

Derek could hardly breath. His mind raced to assemble the pieces of what had just happened, to formulate them into some sort of data he could actually process. What had he just witnessed? "Are you alright?" he asked.

Sandra had rolled off of him now, and was sitting upright on the verge beside him. "DO I FUCKING LOOK ALRIGHT?" she snapped, just about managing to compose the words, before her deep sobs continued.

"What happened?" Derek asked, just about the only question that really mattered.

Sandra shook her head. She took a breath, composed herself. Her body was shaking. "Something… It came out of the drain… It took my poor little Toby!"

Feces Of Death

"What was it? A rat perhaps?" It didn't seem likely that a rat might've run from the sewers to attack her dog, to then drag it away. But what else could it possibly have been? Derek *had* seen some fairly sizable rats over the years.

Sandra shook her head once again. "I don't know what it was. It all happened so fast. But… but… Oh, God! It killed Toby! It tore him to shreds!"

Derek didn't know what to say. How could he possibly comfort this woman? She'd lost the only family member she had left. So instead of saying anything, he simply sat there on the ground, his eyes moving between the ragged remains of Toby's collar, and the drain in which the poor creature had died.

What could possibly have done such a thing?

"No, no, no…" Sandra muttered to herself. "Not Toby. Not *my* Toby. You can't have him. He's mine! Toby… Toby… TOBY!"

CHAPTER TWO
Same Shit, Different Day

"Okay," groaned Martin, laid on his back, the cold, uncomfortable tile of Mrs. Cooper's kitchen floor gnawing painfully into his spine. His head was buried in the cupboard beneath the sink, the light of his head-mounted torch shining on the underside of the stainless-steel bowl. "Try that."

Martin had arrived to find water gushing from a pipe somewhere beneath the kitchen worktop, a pool already forming in the middle of the kitchen floor. Like most people, Mrs. Cooper didn't seem to know where the stopcock was located. It was silly really; had she only taken the time to find where it was beforehand, she'd have been able to shut off the water quickly. As she hadn't, the kitchen was now flooded, and the base units of her cupboards had taken some pretty substantial damage.

But none of that was his concern; he was only here to fix the leak.

He listened as Mrs. Cooper turned the tap on, the stiff copper grinding as the faucet loosened. And then came the gurgling from the pipes as the water pressure began to build. And then he heard the water, rushing through the pipes. The faucet sputtered once or twice, but then the water was flowing freely. Martin took another moment to listen to it cascading down the plughole, and running away through the waste pipe, in the opposite direction to that in which it had just come.

Most importantly, the leak was no more.

Martin grunted as he pushed himself out of the cupboard. Today was his birthday; he'd just turned twenty-seven, although he sometimes felt as if he were seventy-two. "Looks like that's done the trick," he said, smiling up at the old lady towering over him. In all actuality, she was only about five feet tall, but with Martin flat on his back, she might as well have been a giant.

"Oh, thank you," said Mrs. Cooper. "I don't know what I would have done without you."

"Don't mention it," Martin said, as he pulled himself up on the worktop, heaving himself back up to his feet. "All in a day's work."

Martin was a plumber. He worked for EcoPlumb, one of the country's largest independent domestic plumbing contractors. Most of his work took him into people's homes, fixing leaks, or installing new furniture and hardware. For the most part, he enjoyed his job. He liked meeting new people. Sometimes, he'd get assigned a job that would take him into some very nice homes, owned by very rich people. David – his boss – trusted him with those jobs, as he knew that Martin would do a good job, and that he'd be entirely polite and courteous. He wouldn't do anything to bring the company into any kind of disrepute. And those were his favourite jobs; he enjoyed getting to snoop around their houses, to see how the other half lived.

EcoPlumb were a decent firm to work for, and David was a decent boss. Things could always be better, of course, but as things stood, they could also be a hell of a lot worse.

Mrs. Cooper was one of those wealthy customers, the widow of some big-time lawyer, who'd died just a few years ago, at the ripe old age of ninety-three. It seemed to Martin that he'd been to Mrs. Cooper's home at least a dozen times since then. Oftentimes, it was for very minor things, things that even an apprentice could fix. It didn't require somebody of Martin's expertise. But Martin didn't mind; again, he quite enjoyed it. Mrs. Cooper would always spoil him, plying him with carrot cake and cups of tea. Martin would always hang around a little while after the job was done, just to talk to her. It seemed to him that this was all she really wanted. Perhaps she caused some these problems on purpose, just so she could call somebody out, just so she could have a little company.

Martin couldn't hang around for long today though; no sooner had he repaired the leak, then his phone was ringing.

It was David.

Martin waved an apologetic hand towards Mrs. Cooper, before answering the call. "Hey, David," he said, cheerfully. "What can I do for you?"

"You finished at the Cooper place yet?" asked David, dispensing with any unnecessary pleasantries. If anything, Martin imagined that he sounded a little flustered.

"I'm just finishing up right now," Martin answered. "Why? What's wrong?"

"Nothing's *wrong*," said David, although, to Martin, that sounded like a lie. "I'm just up to my goddamn eyeballs in call-outs right now. I need you to get to the next job for me."

David definitely sounded stressed. "Sure. Yeah. No problem. Where am I going?"

"In town. The address is two-four-six, Pratchett Road."

"Yeah, I know it. I can be there in twenty minutes. What's the job?"

"Just a repair. Don't worry about it. Just let me know how you get on, okay?"

"You got it," said Martin. He was about to ask for more detail in regards to what the job entailed – it wasn't like David to be so vague – but then he heard the line go dead, David having hung up without even so much as a 'goodbye'. Not that this was any kind of a problem at all – David *was* a busy man after all – but this level of rudeness was somewhat out of character for him.

He was definitely stressed.

Martin returned his phone to the front pocket of his work trousers. "Sorry," he said, returning his attention to Mrs. Cooper. "But I need to shoot. It sounds like we've got a big job on."

"Oh," said Mrs. Cooper, her disappointment clearly evident. "You can't stay for some cake? I baked brownies."

"No, sorry. I wish I could, believe me. But it sounds like this job is urgent."

Mrs. Cooper nodded understandingly. "Okay," she said. "Well, hopefully I'll see you again soon."

Martin smiled. "Hopefully not too soon. If I end up back here, that means I'm not doing my job right."

"This is an old house. There are plenty of problems with the plumbing."

"Of course. If you ever have any issues, you know who to call."

"I most certainly do. Here, take this with you." Mrs. Cooper placed a slice of her homemade chocolate brownie into a tupperware container and held it out for Martin to take.

"Thank you," said Martin. And with that, he made his way to the front door, his tool bag in one hand and his brownie containing tupperware in the other.

Martin knew exactly where Pratchett Road was; he'd done numerous jobs there over the years. He arrived a few minutes early, so he took a moment to sit in his van and eat the cake so generously gifted to him by Mrs. Cooper. As he'd expected it would be, it was delicious.

A few moments later, he made his way to the front door of the property; a modern, three-storey townhouse, on a fairly crowded estate. He knocked on the door and waited. A few moments passed before a lady answered. "Are you the plumber?" she asked, the moment they locked eyes.

"I am, yes," said Martin. "I understand you have a problem you need me to look at."

"Yes, that's right. Please, come on in."

Inside the house, Martin was greeted by a man; the woman's partner, no doubt. He held out his hand. "Thanks for coming on such short notice," he said, as Martin shook his hand, the man's grip excessively

Feces Of Death

firm. "I've tried to sort the problem myself, but I just can't figure out what's causing it."

"That's alright," said Martin. In his experience, it was *never* good when people tried to fix their own problems; they always managed to make things worse. "I'm sure we can find out what's going on. I'm sorry - but I don't *actually* know what your issue is."

"Ah," said the man, an embarrassed expression spreading awkwardly across his face. "Well, our toilet seems to have backed up somewhat."

"Right..."

"Don't forget to tell him about the thing," said the lady.

"Now, Bev," said the man. "We don't know for sure there was a '*thing*'."

"But you said..."

"I know what I said, but I can't be sure."

Martin found himself growing increasingly confused by what this couple were now bickering about. "What '*thing*'?" he asked, almost certain that it wasn't going to be relevant to his fixing their plumbing issue.

But then, he hadn't expected the man to say what he said next.

"I'm pretty sure I saw something in the toilet," the man said, looking all the more flustered now. "It was moving around in all the... the shit. At least, I think there was something moving in there..."

Now Martin understood why David had been so coy on the phone; nobody liked these sorts of jobs. Digging around through other people's excrement was nobody's idea of a good time (not that digging around through *one's own* excrement would be considered much fun either). But, this issue with the thing moving inside the toilet bowl… "Sounds like it could have been a rat," he said, trying his best to make this sound like a common occurrence. It wasn't, of course. But it did happen *sometimes*. It wasn't beyond the realms of possibility that a rat had crawled up from the sewers and into their toilet. "If there's a blockage in the system somewhere, and a rat couldn't get through, then it's entirely possible that they could've accidentally found their way up here."

"Well that's just great!" huffed the man. "Rats! That's all we need!"

"I'm sure it's not that bad, John!" The lady said to her husband, before turning her attention back to Martin – "Is it?"

Martin offered a comforting smile. "Oh, no. I wouldn't have thought so. It will only be one rat… if it even *is* a rat. We're not talking about some kind of infestation here."

"Right," said the man, whose name Martin now knew to be John. "Exactly. It's probably nothing, right? I probably just imagined it."

Martin nodded in agreement. He hadn't wanted to say so, for fear of offending the customer, but the truth was that he *did* believe John's mind was most likely playing tricks on him. "Yeah," he said. "Probably."

The couple led Martin upstairs and into the bathroom. It was a nice room, having recently been remodelled. There was a large jacuzzi bathtub, with an overhead shower. There was a double vanity unit, with two basins and a wide mirror affixed to the wall behind. The walls were stone effect panels – very modern. Patterned tiles lined the floor.

Feces Of Death

And there, in the corner of the room, was the main offender – the lavatory.

"Okay," said Martin, as he strutted confidently across the room. "Let's see what we're dealing with then." The porcelain bowl was filled to the brim with grunge, flakes of fecal matter floating on the surface of the dirty water, entwined with clumps of saturated tissue paper.

"I did try to unblock it myself," said John, apologetically. "But I couldn't shift it."

"Don't worry," said Martin. "I've seen worse." That was true; he *had* seen worse. *Much* worse.

"Do you think you can fix it?" asked Bev.

"I'm sure I can get *this* cleared. But whether I can fix the root cause really depends on a few things. You say you saw a rat in here?" Martin was now considering the possibility that there may have been a rat in here, after all.

"I saw *something*," said John. "I'm sure of it. I just don't know *what* it was."

"Well," said Martin. "Assuming it *was* a rat - and I can't think of anything else it *might have* been - then that means that, most likely, the cause of the blockage is actually somewhere outside of your property. That's the only way a rat could have been driven out of the sewers and into here. Unless it was already in your system, of course, but that's unlikely. So what that does mean, is that this would actually be a council problem – something backing up the system, something they really ought to be fixing themselves."

"Surely that will take forever," said John.

Martin shrugged his shoulders. "It shouldn't. They're normally pretty responsive to these sorts of things. They know it'll get quite costly for them if they don't act fast."

"If you say so."

Martin continued – "So, what I'll do right now, is I'll get this cleared so at least you've got a usable toilet, then I'll make some calls, see if we can't get the sewerage guys to look into this ASAP, okay?"

"Yeah. I guess so."

Bev was seemingly much more grateful. "That would be wonderful," she said. "Thank you."

Martin got to work.

CHAPTER THREE
Help The Homeless

Jasper waited patiently in line, just like all the other vagrants. Unlike all those other tramps, Jasper didn't really *deserve* to be homeless. It wasn't his fault that he had nowhere to go. It hadn't always been like this.

Once upon a time, Jasper had been your ordinary, run-of-the-mill member of society. Back then, he'd had a job in a warehouse, driving a forklift truck. He had a wife and a young son. They lived in a nice apartment, in a nice part of town. Back then, his life had been pretty great.

But something was changing at home. He could feel something brewing in the air. It was as if there was a palpable tension thickening the oxygen that filled his lungs, tasting bitter as it slipped down his trachea.

It didn't take long for him to realise just what it was that had caused this; it was his wife, Chelsea.

She was a good-looking girl, always had been. He'd felt so lucky when he'd actually managed to hook up with her. And when she actually agreed to marry him… Jasper couldn't imagine anything that might've felt better. Everybody always told him that he was punching well above his weight, and the truth was that he was inclined to agree.

They'd been married for nearly five years before Bertie had come along. Bertie was now nearly five himself. Chelsea had never really wanted kids. Jasper had though, but this was something he was willing to sacrifice in order to be with the love of his life. When Chelsea had found out she was pregnant, she had wanted to get an abortion. Jasper had begged her not to, begged her to give parenthood a shot. She'd told him that this wasn't what she wanted from her life. But Jasper had continued to plead with her, until she finally succumbed.

Jasper knew that Chelsea resented him for this. She loved Bertie, of course; she would do *anything* for him.

Except for remaining faithful to his father.

Jasper didn't know what he'd done to drive her into the arms of another man. He must've done *something*. It couldn't have just been down to his insistence on their raising Bertie together. That child had brought them both so much joy.

Whatever it was, it didn't matter now. Chelsea was gone. She'd left Jasper, and she had taken Bertie with her.

Jasper had turned to drink soon after, thinking, perhaps, that he might be able to find the solution to his problems in the bottom of an empty bottle of Jack Daniels. The thing with that idea was this: a bottle of Jack Daniels never *arrives* empty – one has to drink the contents first, in order to find those elusive answers hidden within. Of course, by the time all the liquor was gone, so was Jasper's memory, along with the question, the answer for which he'd been searching.

Still, Jasper tried tirelessly, until his ill-conceived pursuit of some tiny shred of happiness had ended up costing him his job. Apparently, driving a forklift truck while inebriated was entirely unacceptable.

With no money coming in, all his savings were gone soon after.

Then they took his house.

Now Jasper lived on the streets, his nights spent cold and alone, hidden away in some shop doorway, huddled in a pile of dirty, flea-ridden blankets, most of which he'd managed to salvage from a recycling container in the local supermarket car park. It was here that he found most of the clothes he was now wearing, too. There was some good stuff in there. It wasn't meant for him, of course; it was supposed to be taken to one of the local charity shops, to be sold, the money raised used to support people *like* him. As such, he considered his theft of this clothing to hardly be a crime at all; he was simply cutting out the middleman.

And now he was standing in line, waiting patiently for his turn to collect the bowl of lukewarm soup that the homeless outreach would provide to him for lunch. Jasper appreciated it, truly. If it wasn't for them, he might not eat all day. The feeling of warm food in his belly was always a welcome one. But what Jasper really hungered for was something that none of the charities would ever provide.

Alcohol.

Jasper knew he was addicted. He knew that this disease had a hold of him now, and that there was little to be done about it. But without alcohol, Jasper felt as though he might as well be dead. He felt as if he *were* dead. He only ever really felt alive when he was intoxicated.

Although the money he managed to scrounge from the good-hearted, hardworking members of society amounted to next to nothing, every penny was spent on booze. Today, he had just about enough to buy himself a cheap bottle of gin. He didn't like the stuff, but it was strong enough to get him plastered, and keep him that way for a full twenty-four hours. As such, that was exactly what he intended to buy.

When his turn came around, he approached the table confidently. Two young women were there – one blonde, one brunette – both of whom were wearing red hi-viz jackets. They were pretty girls, both in their early twenties, no doubt. Both had pretty eyes and clean, smooth skin. Oh boy, what he'd give for a night with either of them!

The blonde girl smiled, greeting Japer kindly. "Hi there," she said. "And how are you today?"

Jasper smiled in return, not caring that his teeth were black, and that his breath doubtlessly smelled of death. "I'm good," he said, wondering just how repugnant these two girls must find him.

"Would you like some soup?" asked the other girl. "And a coffee?"

"Yes, please."

Smiling effortlessly the entire time, the two girls prepared Jasper's lunch, one of them spooning tomato soup from a large kettle and into a disposable bowl, while the other poured coffee in a paper cup.

Feces Of Death

Jasper took both and went on his way, but not before looking the two girls over once more, knowing that he'd masturbate to his memory of them later on.

But not before he'd had his gin.

Jasper drank back the soup and disposed of the bowl into a bin. He then drank the coffee. It was so hot it damn-near burned his tongue. But it felt good in his belly, warming him from the inside out.

He then made his way along the street and into the off licence.

"Good afternoon, Jasper," said the man behind the counter. He knew Jasper by name, as Jasper was undoubtedly his best customer; he came here every day to procure his alcohol. "I wasn't sure I'd see you today, my friend. I thought you might be dead."

Jasper laughed. "Not dead," he said. "At least, I don't *think* I'm dead."

"Well, I'm pretty sure you're here talking to me, so unless you're some kind of zombie, I think you're okay."

"That's good to know." Jasper shuffled his way through the store, to where the stronger spirits were kept, along the back wall. He found the cheapest bottle of gin, and plucked a bottle from the shelf. He then paid and left.

"See you tomorrow, my friend," said the shopkeeper, as Jasper left the store, tucking the bottle under his jacket, so that the other vagrants wouldn't notice.

From there, Jasper made his way into the park. It was a large open expanse, a number of grassy fields, separated by rows of trees, a footpath snaking its way from one side to the other. Jasper had his favourite spot in which to get drunk. There was a bench at the edge of the park, for the most part hidden from the areas that saw the most footfall. This was *his* bench. He could get some privacy there, and he could enjoy his gin.

But there was somebody there today, sitting on his bench. It was a woman. Jasper could tell immediately that, like him, she was homeless. Her face was gaunt, her skin sallow and stretched across her cheekbones. Red pimples spotted her forehead. Her lips were dry and chapped.

She was an addict, just like Jasper, although he expected she was into some heavier shit than just alcohol.

"Got any change?" the woman asked, as Jasper approached.

"Do I look like I've got any change?" Jasper replied, finding himself annoyed at the fact that this bitch was sitting in *his* spot.

"Fuck… You on the streets too?"

Jasper nodded.

"Yeah…That's some tough shit, huh?"

"Yep. Sure is." Jasper took a seat on the bench, beside the woman. He looked at her face and decided it was almost impossible to tell how old she was; she looked like some ancient hag, although it was entirely possible she was young, her addiction having done a number on her.

"Got anythin' to eat?" the woman asked.

"Nope," Jasper said, sternly.

"Got anythin' to drink?"

"Not for you, I don't," Jasper sighed, knowing that if he were to take out his bottle now, this woman would surely expect him to share. That wasn't something he was even willing to consider.

But the woman wouldn't drop it. "Is that a yes?" she said, leaning forward, trying to lock eyes with Jasper.

"It's a *'no'*," he said. "Nothing. For. You."

"You don't gotta be so tight," scoffed the woman. "What if I let you fuck me? Then do I get a drink?"

Jasper looked the woman in the eye. He wasn't sure if she was serious or not. This wasn't a woman he would normally have wanted to sleep with. Chelsea has been gorgeous; this woman was nothing of the sort. But Jasper hadn't had sex in years, and beggars can't be choosers. "You serious?" he asked.

The woman nodded. "Whatcha got?"

Jasper pulled the bottle of gin out from under his jacket.

The woman's eyes seemed to light up. Jasper could see a happiness in them, something that, all of a sudden, made her look immensely beautiful. "Very nice," said the woman, licking her lips. "Come on. I know a place we can go. It's very private. Nobody will interrupt us. We can drink that liquor and maybe have a little fun while we're at it."

"Lead the way," said Jasper, his dick itching now, the juice between this bitch's legs suddenly more desirable than the juice in the bottle.

The woman stood from the bench. With a nod of her head, she urged Jasper to follow. Obediently, Jasper stood and followed the woman as she led him out of the park, through the trees and down a steep slope, following the path carved by a narrow stream.

The stream babbled along until it split off in two directions – one, seeming to continue on, possibly for all eternity; the other, leading off to the left, into a large sewer tunnel, buried deep into the hillside.

"This way," said the woman, directing Jasper towards the tunnel.

"In there?" asked Jasper, hardly able to believe that this was where the woman was taking him. The tunnel was actually a large concrete tube, seemingly punching a hole into the centre of the earth. A series of iron bars ran top to bottom, the intention being to keep people from entering. But they were rusted through, twisted and separated, more than enough for a person to squeeze through. Beyond these bars, the tunnel faded away into the darkness.

"You ain't scared, are you," laughed the woman. "Don't you worry about nothin'. I'll be right behind you."

Jasper was apprehensive. But he was also as horny as fuck, and couldn't wait to blow his load in the woman's juicy slit. He didn't even care if she was diseased; he was going in bareback. Cautiously, he entered the sewer pipe.

It smelled bad in there, a sour scent of ammonia hanging in the air. The water felt thick and sludgy underfoot, but Jasper put this down to his overactive imagination. There were a number of discarded car tyres and overturned crates strewn around the pipe. A thick layer of cardboard had been laid to one side, part way into the water. The bottom layers were saturated, but the top seemed to be relatively dry. There was a duvet dumped here too, making it clear that somebody – this woman, presumably – had been sleeping here.

Feces Of Death

Jasper turned to face the woman, who had entered the tunnel behind him. "So," she smirked. "You like what I've done with the place?"

"Yeah," snorted Jasper. "Very homely."

The woman laughed. She smiled, running her tongue over her crooked teeth. Were she a better-looking woman, Jasper may have found this to be somewhat seductive. But she wasn't, yet Jasper still failed to be repulsed; his prick yearned to feel the warmth of her snatch.

The woman pushed in close. Standing on her tiptoes, her hands on Jasper's shoulders, she kissed him. Jasper reciprocated, allowing his tongue to slide into her mouth, her vile saliva running over his taste buds.

Despite how rancid her mouth tasted, Jasper didn't try to stop. To the contrary – he ran his hands over her body, kneading her soft, sagging breasts through the thin material of the t-shirt she was wearing, the soft flesh feeling like two deflated footballs.

The woman reached into Jasper's trousers and found him to already be hard. She stroked the length of his member, her grip firm, her calloused fingertips rough against the delicate skin that surrounded his urethra.

"So," the woman whispered. "How about that drink?"

Jasper didn't protest as the woman took the bottle of gin from him and used her teeth to unscrew the cap, her one hand never leaving the confines of his pants.

It felt so good. Jasper had yearned for the touch of a woman for so long. He was surprised that he didn't climax within seconds.

The woman slicked her lips with her tongue and took a long swig from the bottle. She then handed it back to Jasper. Jasper took a long pull himself, thankful for the sweet taste that seemingly calmed the anxiety brewing in his gut.

And then the woman was stroking him once more, having now released his member from the confines of his piss-stained jogging bottoms, the air cool against the tip.

It felt good – it felt *amazing* – but there was something bothering Jasper, something that was putting him off his stride. It was *this place*. He didn't like it. There was no way he could fuck this woman in the filth. And the putrid stench of shit and piss was almost unbearable. "You think we could go somewhere else?" he asked the woman.

"Are you going to book us into a fancy hotel?" the woman laughed, smiling sarcastically.

"No. But… This place is fucking disgusting." Jasper would've sworn that the smell was getting worse by the second.

And then there was a noise. Something scurrying, perhaps, splashing in the filthy mire that drifted deep into the darkness of the sewer tunnels. But not rats; Jasper knew the sound of rats – he'd spent more than enough time around them over the past few years, enough that he would recognise the pitter-patter of their feet anywhere. So, what then? A friend had once told Jasper of how somebody had once flushed a baby alligator down the toilet. The alligator had survived, and had gone on to grow to enormous proportions. Jasper doubted that to be true, however. Still, there was something down there, hidden in the darkness. "What was that?" Jasper muttered.

"I don't know," said the woman, apparently much less concerned than Jasper. She took another swig of the gin. "Who cares?"

But there was that noise again. Definitely not rats. Something bigger. A man, perhaps. Did they need help?

A similar thought must've crossed the woman's mind, as she turned to peer into the darkness. "Hello?" she called. "Anybody there?" She took a step deeper into the tunnel.

Jasper followed. "What do you think it is?"

The woman shrugged her shoulders. "There's loads of perverts 'round here. Probably somebody wantin' to watch us fuck each other's brains out." She took another step forward, then called into the darkness – "Hey! Who's down there? Come on out. Maybe I'll let you fuck me too."

There was the noise again, closer now. Closer still, moving through the stagnant sewer water.

The woman looked back over her shoulder, to where Jasper was waiting. "See," she whispered, as if she didn't want the stranger hiding in the darkness to hear her. She raised an eyebrow, a sly smile plastered to her face. "Perverts - they'll do anythin' if they think they might get their dick sucked."

Jasper couldn't help but share in her amusement.

But then something sprang from the darkness, a shape, dark in colour, a man, perhaps, but maybe not. It was all over in a flash, too quick for Jasper's fragile mind to contemplate just what it was he was seeing. Arms, thick and wet, wrapped around the woman's waist, dragging her into the depths of the sewer. And she was screaming! Her agonised howls echoed from the concrete walls of the tunnel.

Jasper couldn't move. The terror he felt in his bones had anchored him to the spot. He could feel his jaw trembling, his arms and legs growing weak. He knew he should run. He knew he needed to get out of there. But his body refused to budge, not even an inch. "H… hello?" he muttered, barely even a whisper.

The woman emerged from the darkness on her hands and knees. She scrambled forward quickly, before collapsing face first into the manky stream of pisswater that flowed into the sewer. Her skin was filthy, and her hair was thick with excrement. And she was bleeding, a ragged chunk of flesh torn from her cheek, revealing her crooked, rotten teeth embedded in the gum below. She reached out with one hand. The skin of her hand had been shredded. Her index finger had been torn off completely, bone protruding from the ragged stump.

It was then that Jasper ran.

But he didn't get far.

Something grabbed him by the ankle, taking his legs out from under him. And then he was being dragged into the darkness of the sewer, screaming as something bit into his calf muscle, digging all the way down to the bone. He could feel the meat of his leg being pulled from his tibia, a wave of insufferable torment burning through his body. He felt the ligaments of his knee give way, his skin tearing as his entire lower leg became detached.

Feces Of Death

As he died, Jasper could only think about one thing: the stench down there was terrible.

And it was getting worse.

CHAPTER FOUR
No Job Too Big

Martin was able to unblock the toilet without too much hassle. In the end, all it had taken was a little old-fashioned elbow grease. Thankfully, he hadn't needed to dismantle any of the plumbing; doing so almost certainly would've caused a horrendous mess – one which he himself would've been liable to clean up. As it so happened, it hadn't taken much effort to dislodge whatever it was that had clogged the u-bend.

Perhaps John hadn't tried quite as hard as he'd made out, to clear the blockage himself.

This was a thought that Martin kept to himself. Bev had thanked him as he'd left their house, telling him that she hoped the problem would be fixed soon enough. Martin assured her that he'd get on to the council as soon as he arrived back at the office, and get them to look into it.

And then he was back in his van, heading back to the office, ready to make the call he'd promised Bev he'd make just a few short moments ago.

But he never made it to the office. Just a few hundred yards up the road, his phone was ringing once again.

It was David.

"Hello," said Martin, as he answered the phone, using his shoulder to clamp the handset to his ear, allowing him to keep both hands on the steering wheel.

"I've got another job for you, if you're available," said David.

It briefly crossed Martin's mind that perhaps he ought to say that he *wasn't* available, as it just so happened. Perhaps he ought to lie, tell David that he was still at his previous job, tell him that he didn't expect to finish there for another forty-five minutes or so. He knew that this was exactly what some of his co-workers would do. But that wasn't Martin's style. He was an honest, hard-working man; no way could he lie to his boss. "It's not another blockage is it?" he asked. "I've just been up to my elbows in shit - I could really do with a break right now."

"I'm not sure," said David. "It might be a blockage. I don't know. I need you to go check it out for me."

Martin sighed. The last thing he needed was to be digging through any more crap. "Fine," he said. "Where's it at?"

"Actually, it's just a few streets down from your last job," David informed him.

"Really? I've just left that place. Where am I going?"

David gave him the address, and Martin pulled up outside the property just a few minutes later.

As Martin made his way along the path towards the front door, his phone once again began to ring. He half expected it to be David once again, fretting as usual, over something entirely trivial. He dug the phone from his pocket and checked the screen. Thankfully, it wasn't David.

It was Emily.

"Hey, birthday boy!" Emily said, as Martin answered the phone. "How's work? They haven't got you working too hard, I hope?"

Martin couldn't help but smile. He and Emily had been together for nearly eight years now, having met back when they were both in college. She had been studying nursing, while he had been working towards his plumbing qualifications. Emily was beautiful, with long blonde hair and the most amazingly deep blue eyes. Martin was rough and ready, with thick stubble and a shaved head. The truth was, he wasn't quite sure how he'd managed to end up with her; she was way out of his league. "No more than usual," Martin said.

"What time do you think you'll be finished today?"

Martin checked his watch. It had already passed three in the afternoon. He *had* hoped to finish up early, what with it being his birthday and all, but, depending on how this next job went, it didn't seem like that would be the case. "I'm not sure. Soon, hopefully."

"Okay. Well, I've got us steak for dinner, and there's a chilled bottle of rosé waiting in the fridge."

"That sounds amazing."

Feces Of Death

"Yep. And then I've got you something extra special for dessert." Emily spoke seductively, a flirtatious tone to her voice.

"Oh, really? What?"

"You'll just have to wait and see, won't you?"

Martin couldn't help but laugh. "Okay. I'll look forward to it."

"Alright. I'll see you later, okay? I love you."

"I love you, too."

"Alright. Bye"

"Bye."

Martin hung up the phone and returned it to his pocket. He was at the front door then. He pressed the doorbell and waited. A few moments later, a man answered the door. He was young, with a scruffy, dishevelled look about him. He wore glasses and had curly hair hanging down over his forehead. "Can I help you?" he said.

"I believe you're in need of a plumber?" Martin said, thinking that it should've been obvious that this was what he was here for.

"You're the plumber?" the young man asked.

Martin nodded.

"Oh. Right. That was quick! Come on in." The man swung his arm wide, ushering Martin inside the house. "It's a bit of a mess, I'm afraid. I'm not sure how this has happened, but my toilet is completely blocked."

Fan-fucking-tastic, thought Martin. "That's okay. I deal with this sort of thing every day. I very much doubt it'll be anything I haven't seen before."

Thankfully, as the man led Martin into the bathroom, he saw that, in actual fact, it wasn't anywhere near as bad as the last place. Although the water had filled the bowl, and had already spilled over the sides, flooding the linoleum, at least it was relatively clean.

Grateful for this small mercy, Martin puffed out his cheeks. "Alright. Let's get this sorted."

Much like the last place, the blockage – whatever it had just so happened to be – had cleared with relative ease. The young man had thanked him, and Martin had gone on his way.

Back outside, Martin checked the time once again. It was now 4p.m. - Martin wanted to get back to the office, make that call to the council, and call it a day. He opened up the back of his van and dropped his toolbox inside, shifting aside a bundle of pipes and a cluster of fittings that had been rattling around loose for more than a week now.

"Hey!" a voice called from somewhere behind, as Martin had been climbing into the driver's seat. He stooped and looked back.

Another man was walking speedily towards him, a purposeful look on his face. "Are you a plumber?" the man asked as he neared.

Martin looked back at the EcoPlumb logo emblazoned on the side of his van. There was no way he could get away with claiming he *wasn't* a plumber, was there? "I am, yes," he sighed, knowing that this question was a loaded one – one which would undoubtedly lead to more work for him to do.

"Oh, great!" said the man. "Thank God you're here! I don't know if this is anything to do with whatever problem you've just fixed in there, but I've got a problem too. I was just wondering if you could take a look."

Feces Of Death

A feeling in Martin's gut told him that he already knew what this guy's problem was. "Let me guess - your toilet is blocked?"

"Got it in one."

It didn't make much sense, but it seemed unlikely that there would be three unrelated blockages in such close proximity to one another; they *had to be* connected, it was too much of a coincidence for them to not be. But what could have caused it? Martin had no idea; that was for the sewer company to figure out. Still, he'd need to report what he'd found.

"So?" asked the man. "Can you take a look for me?"

"Yeah, sure," replied Martin. "But I need to make a phone call first. Just give me a minute, okay? You head back inside, and I'll meet you there."

"Okay. Thanks."

Martin watched as the man returned to his house. He then pulled his phone from his pocket once again, and dialled the number of the office.

***

The fucking phone hadn't stopped ringing all fucking day, and the sound of it was really starting to drive David insane. This wasn't what he'd signed up for. When he'd been promoted to area manager, he hadn't realised that he was agreeing to become some kind of a glorified desk jockey. All he seemed to do nowadays was answer the phone and delegate jobs to the eighty-four blokes he had working under him.

Still, he supposed the additional pay made it all worthwhile. And there was no getting away from the fact that this was a much less strenuous job.

Not that this was necessarily a good thing; David had put on a fair amount of weight over the past few years that he'd been doing this job. He was getting less exercise, and the temptation to sit at his desk snacking all day was just too great. Sometimes he wished he were still out on the road, still getting his hands dirty.

Especially on days like today.

David arrived in the office that morning to a grand total of seventeen voicemails, each one requesting an emergency visit from one of his engineers. That number in and of itself was extraordinary; there were normally one or two voicemails waiting for him each morning, but *never* so many.

And since then, the calls hadn't stopped.

They were coming from all over town. At least two-hundred incidents so far, of people reporting that their toilets were blocked, or that their drains were backing up.

It was bizarre. David had never known anything like it. For the life of him, he couldn't even comprehend what would cause such a thing. There had to be some sort of massive failure within the sewer system itself.

David had once read an article about '*fatbergs*' – giant mounds of kitchen fat and soaps and all the other human waste products that got flushed down the drains when they really ought to not have. They could grow to be several metres in diameter and weigh several tonnes. On occasion, they got so big that they blocked entire sewer inlets. Perhaps that's what this was; some massive mountain of crap obstructing the sewer pipes, disrupting the proper flow of the sewerage.

Whatever it was, David needed it fixed ASAP – he couldn't keep sending his guys out to these jobs, not when there was little they could do to fix the root cause of the problem itself.

As such, David had already been onto the local council about it. They had put him in contact with a guy named Stanley Bishop, one of the engineering managers over at the sewer processing plant.

Stanley had sounded both sympathetic and disinterested, all at the same time. He'd said they knew there was a problem somewhere within the network, and that they were looking into it. He couldn't tell David just *what* the problem was, as he had no idea himself. He had promised to keep David updated, should any new information come to light.

That was several hours ago now, and David hadn't heard anything since.

The phone was ringing again. David sighed, entirely exasperated. "EcoPlumb," he said, as he answered the call. "How can we help?"

"Hey, David," said Martin, a voice David was genuinely glad to hear. "What's going on? I've got multiple blockages all on the same street. This can't be coincidental - they must be related somehow."

"Yeah, I know," said David. "But it's not just one street - it's all over town." David didn't mind telling Martin everything he knew. Martin was a good man, one of his best engineers. Not only that, but he was a good friend also. The two of them used to be inseparable. They had known each other since middle school. They had gone to college together, and had gained their qualifications at the same time. They had both then started working for EcoPlumb at the same time. When the management position had become available (when their former boss had died in a horrific car accident), David had only gotten the job over Martin because he was better at brown-nosing the higher-ups.

"It's got to be something to do with the sewers," said Martin.

"I know. I've already connected all the dots. The guy I spoke to at the processing plant seemed to be pretty much clueless."

The line went silent for a few extended moments, before Martin said – "Well, I guess there's nothing more I can do. I'm going to call it a day, okay? Emily's cooking me steak as a special treat for my birthday."

David had completely forgotten that it was Martin's birthday. "Oh, shit - sorry, man. I forgot. We'll have to go out for some drinks some time soon."

"Yeah. We should definitely do that."

"Alright. Well - you get yourself home. Have a good evening - I'm sure there'll be plenty of shit for you to get stuck into tomorrow."

Martin laughed. "Not literally, I hope!"

Laughing, David ended the call. He decided to try the processing plant again, to see if they had any new information. He dialled the number he'd been given earlier that day.

David listened to the phone ringing for what almost felt like an hour. Just as he was about to give up, an annoyed voice answered. "Hello?"

"Oh, good evening," said David, as politely as possible. "Could I possibly speak to Stanley Bishop, please?"

"Speaking," said the voice at the other end of the line.

"Ah, Stanley. My name's David, I'm calling from EcoPlumb. We spoke earlier about a possible blockage. I was just wondering if you had any updates for me."

"No," grunted Stanley, sounding entirely pissed off. "I don't. I've got a couple guys heading down there right now, to see what they can find. That's all I can tell you right now. Call back tomorrow." Then, with a CLICK, the line went dead.

CHAPTER FIVE
For The Love Of Sewerage

"You'll never really appreciate the smell of raw sewerage, kid."

Aaron could feel himself frowning. Was that supposed to be ironic? He wasn't quite sure he understood the sentiment. Was he *supposed* to appreciate the smell of raw sewerage? "What do you mean?" he asked the old man.

"What I mean is," said Winston, looking back over his shoulder, one eyebrow raised. "This place stinks of shit. It always stinks of shit, so you best get used to it. The sooner, the better."

Aaron scoffed a laugh. "How long did it take for *you* to get used to it?"

Winston scrunched up his face and shrugged his shoulders. "I don't think I am, not yet."

It hadn't exactly been Aaron's dream job, working in sanitation, but the truth was, so far, he didn't mind it all too much. Granted, he'd only been on the job for a week, so there was plenty of time for him to change his mind. But – so far, so good.

Feces Of Death

Aaron was seventeen. Like most teenagers, he'd never really had any idea what he wanted to do with his life. It was this lack of direction that had led him into this job. Somebody had once told him that the dirtier a job was, the bigger the wage packet at the end of the week. It turned out that you could be very handsomely compensated, if only you were willing to wade through other people's piss and shit for a living. And, for the money, this was something that Aaron was very much willing to do. Again, it wasn't exactly a dream job – not by a long stretch – but there were plenty of worse things he could be doing, he supposed.

Arron had never been afraid of a little hard graft. He was quite happy to get his hands dirty. As a trainee, he was on a lower wage than he might've liked, but he knew that wouldn't last forever. This wasn't a role for which he'd needed any specific qualifications; he could learn on the job, and that suited him perfectly. Within a year or two, he'd be fully qualified, and earning a real wage. Winston was the old boy who had been assigned to show him the ropes.

It seemed that Winston thought the best option was for Aaron to be thrown in at the deep end – quite literally. His first day had seen him waist-deep in the murky sewer water, the foul odour making him gag on numerous occasions. Winston had found this to be highly amusing.

"What exactly is it we're looking for?" Aaron asked, as he climbed down the corroded rungs of the ladder and onto the concrete slab below. He was dressed in his waterproof overalls and his thigh-high rubber boots. The pungent stench of the stagnant water wafted into his nostrils, threatening to make him lose his lunch.

"I ain't too sure, kid," said Winston, following Aaron down the ladder, deep into the vast network of tunnels that ran beneath the town.

Aaron had never asked Winston how old he was, but if he were to hazard a guess, he'd have assumed he was in his late fifties. His face was lined with the deep wrinkles of a man who'd worked tirelessly for the past thirty-something years. He wore glasses and his grey hair was thinning, the wispy strands combed back to assist in hiding his bald spot. He'd been working the sewers since he was a teenager, much like Aaron was now. There was nobody better for Aaron to learn from.

"Well, something *has to be* causing all the drains to be backing up, right?" Aaron looked along the sewer tunnels, the light of the torch mounted to the front of his hard hat dancing in the darkness, bouncing from the slimy, moss-covered walls.

"Yep," said Winston. "That sounds about right. But your guess is as good as mine, kid."

Aaron didn't exactly like the way that Winston continually called him 'kid'. It felt patronising. Still, he never said anything. "So - which way do we go?"

From their current position, there were three tunnels they could possibly follow. None looked any more attractive than the other.

The dull rumble of cars speeding along the streets above filtered through the tunnels, reminding Aaron just how isolated they were down there.

Winston pushed his fingers up under the rim of his hard hat and scratched at his scalp. He shook his head. "Kid - we don't even know *what it is* we're looking for. Any one of these tunnels could be the right one. You pick. Who knows - maybe you might get lucky."

Aaron looked along each of the tunnels in turn. They were all pitch black, each indistinguishable from the next. "That one?" he said, nodding his head towards the middle of the three tunnels.

Winston held out his hand, his palm facing up. "Lead the way."

Aaron took a breath. This was the part he'd found he liked the least. He crouched, placing his right hand onto the concrete. He then stepped down, both feet simultaneously, into the rancid water. His splashing caused a stink to rise from the surface of the water. It was entirely gross, once again threatening to make him gag.

"You okay down there, kid?" smirked Winston, barely able to contain himself.

"Yeah. I'm fine. Just hurry up, will ya?"

Winston laughed. "You should know me by now, kid - I'm not in the habit of rushing anywhere." He sat on the edge of the concrete pad, and slowly lowered himself into the water.

The water was at around mid-thigh on Aaron. A slight current pushed back against him as he waded onward, as if it were trying to prevent him from heading in that direction. Perhaps the sewers themselves were trying to tell him something. As he pushed forward, he held his arms out at his side, perpendicular to his body. Under no circumstances would he allow his hands to dip below the surface of that disgusting, piss-and-shit-infused water. Gloves or no gloves, it just wasn't happening.

Not like Winston. He seemed quite content to allow his latex-clad fingertips to drag along the surface, ripples in the water radiating outward, the minimal light shimmering in every direction.

Aaron didn't know the layout of these tunnels, not like Winston did, not yet. But, at that particular moment, Winston wasn't proving to be much help. The pair of them were walking aimlessly, just hoping that they might randomly stumble across the cause of all the troubles they were having up top. To Aaron, that seemed increasingly unlikely. They had been sent down here without so much as the slightest indication as to what it was they were looking for. When Winston had asked for some sort of a clue, the response had been something along the lines of – *'you'll know it when you see it'*. What good was that?

But then they did find something.

Aaron had been working down in the sewers for less than seven days. During that time, he'd decided that the worst thing about the sewers was the rats. They were huge, with fat, furry bodies, and long, scabby tails. They were everywhere, thousands of them, swarming through the tunnels, climbing the pipes, swimming through the water. Truth be told, that was the main reason that Aaron wouldn't let his hands sit in the water; if his fingers happened to brush up against the fat, furry body of one of those foul creatures, he might just drop a turd in his pants.

But never before had he seen so many of them in one place. Even Winston seemed to be taken aback by the sheer number of them.

They were all scurrying away, perched on the thin concrete ledge that ran the length of the tunnel, moving in single file. They were heading towards the two men, then ignoring them as they passed. It was if they were evacuating the sewers, desperate to escape from *something* – something into which Aaron and Winston were now heading.

"What the fuck is this?" muttered Aaron, unsure if he'd said it loud enough for Winston to hear, or if he'd said it at all.

Evidently, Winston *had* heard him. "I don't know, kid," said Winston, shaking his head in disbelief. "I ain't never seen anything like this. Not once in the thirty-four years I've been working down here, have I ever seen the rats acting like this."

"It's like they're scared. It's like they're running away from something." There was something unnerving about the way the rodents were behaving. This wasn't the way they normally acted. There was something wrong. Discomfort began to itch at Aaron's bones.

"I don't know, kid. These sewer rats ain't afraid of nothing."

"Well, they're all heading in the opposite direction to us. Maybe we ought to follow their lead…"

"Don't be daft. Keep going. We gotta see what it is that's gotten them spooked."

Aaron couldn't speak for the rats, but he knew that he himself was feeling more than a little 'spooked'. As he led the way through the water, he began to notice dark shapes floating on the surface, bobbing up and down, slowly floating towards him, urged on by the current. One of those shapes floated right by Aaron. He tipped his head forward, so that the light of his head torch would illuminate it.

He gasped, his next breath catching in the back of his throat.

It was the remains of a dead rat. Aaron tried to not look too closely, but even in the slight glimpse he had forced himself to take, he saw that some of the animal's skin had been removed from its face, exposing the tiny skull beneath.

They were all rats. Each and every one of those shapes bobbing along in the water was the corpse of a rat, their fat, bloated bodies mutilated in one way or another.

"Oh my God," said Aaron, his heart racing now. He placed the back of his hand to his mouth, hoping to prevent himself from throwing up. "That's fucking disgusting."

"Yeah," Winston agreed. "I don't like this one bit. Somethin' ain't right."

"You don't say."

Winston passed Aaron, continuing along the tunnel. Aaron shook his head. "Hey! Winston! What are we doing?"

Winston didn't reply.

"Come on, man," said Aaron, slowly inching his way forward, not wanting to drift too far away from Winston. "There's a bunch of dead rats! Surely that's enough to warrant us gettin' the fuck out of here? What about diseases? Whatever killed them, it might just kill us too!"

Winston continued to ignore Aaron.

"*Shit*," Aaron muttered to himself, before following Winston deeper into the sewers.

A few yards on, and Winston stopped. Aaron fell still beside him.

"What the fuck is that?" muttered Aaron.

Feces Of Death

There was something there, ahead of them, amongst the darkness. It looked like some mound of unidentifiable organic matter – an accumulation of fecal matter, perhaps. It was sitting in the water, the crest breaching the surface like an iceberg. Whatever this was, it looked slimy and sticky, mottled green and black and brown. An awful smell emanated from it – far worse than anything Aaron had ever smelled before – like a rancid concoction of dried vomit and decomposing waste.

Aaron wasn't sure if it was just a trick of the light, what with the only source of illumination being the dull, unsteady light of his head torch – itself reflected from the disturbed water, bouncing off the grungy surface of the tunnel – but the thing in the water almost looked as if it was moving. It almost looked as if it were alive. It seemed to be pulsating, as if it were breathing, its outer surface undulating.

"Wh... what is it?" Aaron muttered once again.

Winston shook his head. "I don't know. I big pile of shit, I guess."

"You think this is what we're looking for?"

"I don't think so. Whatever this is, it's not big enough to block any of these tunnels, is it? Maybe some of the smaller pipes, but... I just don't know."

Winston took a step towards the pile of filth. Aaron quickly snatched his arm, stopping him in his tracks. "What are you doing?" he grunted, his voice little more than a whisper.

"I'm gonna go see what it is. Don't be so stupid, kid - whatever it is, it ain't going to kill you." Winston pulled his arm free and continued on through the water.

There was something squirming in Aaron's gut, telling him that this was a bad idea. Despite this, he followed Winston.

More dead rats floated by, some with their flesh removed, others with their limbs removed. One of them even seemed to be missing its head entirely.

Winston approached the dirty mound. Aaron stopped a few yards behind, not wanting to get too close. He tried to convince himself that he wasn't scared, but the truth was he was petrified. A sudden thought crossed his mind that, in actual fact, perhaps working in the sewers wasn't the job for him.

Aaron was still processing this thought when Winston all of a suddenly darted to one side. "Shit!" groaned Winston. "What the fuck?"

"What is it?" said Aaron, his voice wavering.

"I swear to God, somethin' just... What in God's name... Ugghhh!" Winston suddenly disappeared under the water, his arms thrashing as he vanished beneath the surface. And then it was still, the mountain of shit shimmering in the darkness.

Aaron's eyes grew wide. He held his breath. "W... W... Winston?" It felt as if an entire day had passed, the silence swelling, an uncomfortable pressure closing in.

Winston *roared* as he burst out of the water, coughing and spluttering, trying to expel as much of the filthy water from his lungs as possible, while simultaneously sucking in a deep breath.

"Oh my God! Winston!" Aaron bolted forward, his hands outstretched to help his older colleague, the fact that he was now splashing himself with the stagnant water doing little to slow him. He just needed to ensure that Winston was okay.

But Winston *wasn't* okay.

It took a moment for Aaron's eyes to focus, but once they did, he saw that half of Winston's face was destroyed. His lower jaw was missing, his mandible bone having been torn clean off. His lips were missing too, as was the flesh from the tip of his nose. His tongue lapped pointlessly at the air, as blood spewed from the cavernous wound that was once his face, the air escaping his lungs blowing bubbles in the ichor. He reached out to Aaron, begging him for help.

Aaron stumbled back, terrified, ashamed of his unwillingness to help. His feet slipped from below him, and he dropped into the water, the vile liquid washing uninvited down his throat, entering via his nostrils. He twisted his body, scrambling up to his feet, emerging from the water just in time to see something long and thin – black and serpentine – wrap itself around Winston's neck, and drag him back under.

He turned and ran, his long strides fighting their way through the water, itself resisting him, trying to hold him back. His legs felt weak, his muscles spasming uncontrollably, ready to give out beneath him.

And then he felt something brush past his ankles, something swimming through the water, seemingly doing so at great speed. The sensation, the knowledge that there was something down there, in the water with him – something *alive* – sent a feeling of terror coursing through his veins. He froze, his head pounding, his hands raised as if he might somehow be able to defend himself.

But nothing happened.

Not for a few seconds, anyway.

And then there was something emerging from the water, an animal of some kind, like nothing Aaron had ever seen before. And then, before he even knew what was happening, it was on him, slithering over him, engulfing him.

Aaron tried to scream. His mouth opened and the sound began to form. But then there was something in his mouth, forcing its way down his throat. A grotesque flavour slid over his tongue, rancid and bitter, as the malleable substance worked its way down his oesophagus *and* his trachea, filling his stomach and his lungs, respectively.

His insides screamed in agony, as whatever it was that was now inside him squirmed and writhed. And then it was tearing its way out of his body, splitting open his internal organs and ripping through his flesh.

Aaron felt his chest burst open, the meat of his lungs pushing between his ribs, before the bones splintered and shredded his skin.

And then…

Nothing.

CHAPTER SIX
No Place Like Home

Martin did his best to forget about his day, just as he always did. He never liked to think about work anymore than he *had* to. That meant that, as soon as his shift was done, he tried his best to switch off entirely.

Not that this was always possible, of course. Sometimes, switching off was entirely impossible.

Like tonight. Something was still playing on his mind as he walked into his home – the small, two-bedroom townhouse he shared with Emily. There was something unsettling about the day's occurrences, something that just seemed... How best to put it? Out of place

He'd dealt with many a blocked toilet over the years, of course. But, three in one day? Such a thing simply *never* occurred. Not in the *way* they had happened, not so close together. There was something serious going on, Martin was sure of it.

Yet, as soon as he walked through the front door, all memories of the day's events faded to nothing.

Emily was standing there before him in the hallway, her smile brightening the uncomfortable feeling that had been settling in the pit of his stomach. Her hair hung in loose curls over her shoulders. She was wearing a red floral print dress, the skirt hanging just below her knees. "Hey!" she said, beaming cheerily. She approached, and – standing on her tiptoes, hands on his shoulders – kissed him on the cheek.

"Hey, to you too," said Martin. He could feel himself smiling, his cheeks already beginning to ache. Emily was beautiful. He loved her more than anything. No matter how hard his day had been, she was always there with a smile on her face, ready to comfort him, to make him feel worthwhile.

"Come on," said Emily, taking him by the hand and leading him down the hallway, towards the kitchen. "Dinner's almost done."

Martin could smell his dinner cooking, the mouth-watering aroma emanating from the kitchen. "I could really do with a shower first," he said. "I've been up to my elbows in shit all day. I probably stink."

Emily smiled back at him. "You don't stink. And you can shower *after* dinner – I don't want to ruin the steak. You do know how much a nice piece of steak costs nowadays, right?"

Martin laughed. "Okay. Alright. Let me just wash my hands."

"Okay. But be quick about it."

"I will." Martin leaned in and kissed Emily on the lips, letting the delicate touch linger for just a second. "I'll just be two seconds."

Emily continued on into the kitchen, while Martin headed upstairs to the bathroom. It was a

Feces Of Death

modest room, with nice furniture and fixtures, which Martin had been able to acquire at a discounted price, what with his numerous acquaintances in the industry. He liked his bathroom. He probably spent too long in there. But he found it peaceful. He found it comfortable. It was about the only place he could go to just be alone, just for five minutes.

As he stood before the basin, he looked himself over in the mirrored door of the medicine cabinet before him. He wondered if he looked as old as he felt. He looked down at the toilet on his right, thankful that it too hadn't become blocked; he didn't think he could deal with another one today. But the fact remained that there was something unusual about those blockages. Sure, his house was on the other side of the town from where those others had been. But then, David had told him that the blockages had actually occurred all over town – it was just as likely to happen in his own house, as it was anywhere else.

Great. *Just great.*

Still, the toilet wasn't blocked right now, and their drains weren't backed up, and Martin prayed to God that it might stay that way.

Hopefully, the guys at the sewer plant would figure out what the issue was and get it sorted overnight. Martin wasn't much in the mood for another day like today.

What was he doing still thinking about work? It was his birthday, and his girlfriend was downstairs, cooking him dinner. He needed to switch off.

But his head was aching, the beginnings of a migraine forming in the back of his skull. He pulled open the medicine cabinet before him, and sifted through the medicines – antihistamines, antiseptics, laxatives, multivitamins, various topical creams – until he found the painkillers. He popped two of the pills from the packet, dropped them onto his tongue, tipped his head back and swallowed.

Martin ran the tap until the water turned warm. He then washed his hands, hoping that – along with the day's grime that had no doubt accumulated there – he might just wash away those thoughts about work, and sewerage, and blocked toilets, and piss and shit. Thankfully, it seemed to work.

A few moments later, he was back downstairs. He entered the kitchen to find that Emily had set the small, round breakfast table – which sat to one side of the kitchen – with two plates, two wine glasses and a tall, skinny candle, the bright red wax already melting down the stem in thick rivulets, like the blood in those old *Hammer Horror* movies. A bucket of ice contained a bottle of rosé wine. "Oh, wow," he said, genuinely taken aback by the effort Emily had put in. "This looks great!"

Emily stood at the cooker, frying the steak. She looked back over her shoulder, beaming. "Only the best for you," she giggled.

Martin approached her from behind. He placed his hands on her hips and pressed his chest to her back. Emily tipped her head to one side, allowing him to nuzzle her neck, softly kissing her delicate skin.

Emily laughed. "Careful," she said. "I know you like your steak medium-rare. If you distract me, you might end up with it well done!"

"Just so long as you don't cremate it…"

"I'll do my best!"

Feces Of Death

Laughing, Martin headed for the table. There, he took a seat and poured himself a glass of wine. He took a sip, before pouring a second glass for Emily.

Just a few minutes later, Emily had joined him, having set a plate before him, stacked with fries and onion rings and a perfectly cooked sirloin. "Happy birthday," she said, as they clinked their glasses together.

They chatted briefly about their day as they ate. Martin told Emily about the blockages, and about the rat that may or may not have scurried up that one couple's toilet, just as a means of maintaining conversation. He forced himself not to dwell on it, as it was just about the last thing he wanted to talk about. And besides, he was quite content to sit and listen to Emily talk about her day instead. As an A&E nurse, her day would've been infinitely more interesting than his own. She'd been on the night shift, and had not gotten home until after Martin had left for work. Apparently, there had been a pretty nasty RTC during the night, which had left one person dead and three more in the emergency room, one of whom had been in a critical condition. Nobody else had died though, so that had been good news.

After dinner, and with the wine bottle now empty, Emily carried the plates over to the sink and dropped them into the bowl. When she returned to the table, she carried with her a small, gift-wrapped box. She placed it on the table and slid it towards Martin. "Happy birthday," she said once again. "Sorry I didn't give this to you this morning."

"That's okay," laughed Martin, as he started to unwrap the gift. Often, they didn't really see each other in the mornings. Most days, Martin had to start early, as had been the case today. He had been up and out the door by 6:30. Normally, starting early would mean he could also finish early. But not on days like today. He pulled the wrapping from the box, and found it to be bound in some black, faux-leather material. Whatever it was that she had bought him, it must've been expensive.

Martin opened the box to find a watch inside. The body was silver and the strap was brown leather. "Oh my God," he muttered under his breath. "You shouldn't have."

Emily straddled Martin, hooking her legs over his lap. She wrapped her arms around his neck and kissed him deeply, stroking his tongue with her own. She tasted good, the sweet flavour of the wine having lined her mouth. She pulled away. "I know I *shouldn't have*," she smiled. "But I *wanted* to. You always spoil me. I thought it was about time *I* spoiled *you* instead."

"Well," said Martin, unsure if it was happiness that was making him slightly giddy, or whether it was actually the wine. "I can promise you it's very much appreciated."

They kissed again.

This time when they separated, Emily was biting her lower lip seductively. "Are you ready for your shower now?" she asked.

"I thought I might as well have dessert first."

Emily looked down, as if she were almost embarrassed. She always came across as confident, but the truth was that she was actually shyer than she'd ever let on. Her cheeks seemed flushed, possibly due to the wine. "You can have your dessert *in* the shower."

Feces Of Death

Martin smiled. Emily locked eyes with him, her cheeks almost scarlet now. "Oh," said Martin. "Is that so?"

Emily bit her lip once again. She nodded her head.

Martin stood from the chair, lifting Emily with him. She giggled, whooping as he hoisted her up onto his shoulder. "Put me down!" she laughed, playfully batting at his shoulder.

He lowered her to his front, but never fully released his grip. Emily wrapped her legs around his waist, squeezing her thighs into his hips. Martin carried Emily up the stairs this way, kissing her the whole way.

In the bathroom, Emily set the shower running. She then helped Martin out of his clothes. He then obliged her by doing the same. Naked, they cuddled, the warmth of Emily's flesh so exquisite against his own. He allowed his hands to caress her back, his fingertips kneading her soft flesh. He could feel the hard nub of her nipples pressing against his own chest, her pert breasts pressed against his muscular form. He could feel his excitement building; he was already erect by the time Emily guided him into the shower.

There, as the cascading water soaked them both, Emily took his manhood in the palm of her hand and stroked it back and forth. Intense pleasure coursed through his body. Emily lowered herself to her knees, the water soaking her hair, and took him in her mouth. Martin tipped his head back under the water, and sighed.

Martin made love to Emily, her back pressed against the mirror, her weight supported by the vanity unit on which she was sat, her legs wrapped around his waist. They made love a second time on the bed.

They slept naked that night, their soft, warm flesh pressed comfortably together.

CHAPTER SEVEN
Uncomfortable Bowel Movements

John awoke to an agonising cramp in belly, as if somebody had reached inside his chest cavity, and was wringing his stomach like a dirty dishcloth.

As a younger man, he'd always loved spicy food; the hotter the better. But now, as he was getting older, he found that spicy food just wouldn't settle in his stomach; it had a nasty habit of playing havoc with his bowels.

He knew that he shouldn't have gone for the vindaloo. He should've gone for something milder. Then perhaps he wouldn't feel as if a boa constrictor had been inserted into his anus, and was now squeezing the living shit out of his internal organs.

He sat up in the bed, his hands pressing hard against his stomach, in hopes that the pressure might relieve some of the tension he felt there. He imagined that this must be something along the lines of what childbirth must feel like.

He checked the time on the digital alarm clock, which sat on his bedside table. It was 02:13.

Fuck.

He had to get out of bed. He had to get to the bathroom. He was either about to puke, or he was about to shit himself. Neither option was particularly favourable, and if he happened to do either of those things in the bed, then Bev was likely to divorce him.

He looked to his wife, sleeping soundly beside him. She'd never liked spicy foods. Whenever he ordered a takeaway from the local Indian restaurant, she always opted for something bland, something very much English. Normally the omelette, or the roasted chicken with a side of chips. It was ridiculous, really. John didn't understand it. How could she not like curry? They hadn't eaten out at an Indian restaurant in years, as John always found it entirely embarrassing, having to sit with her while she decided on which flavourless, non-Indian option to pick.

Anyway, her having had something so bland meant that her stomach was having no problems whatsoever in digesting whatever it was she had consumed. John's stomach on the other hand, was just about ready to implode.

Taking a breath, John kicked the blanket away and swung his legs out into the frigid air of the bedroom. A sudden and horrifying thought hit him then – the toilet was blocked, wasn't it?

No. That bloke had come by and fixed it earlier that afternoon. He seemed like a good guy, very thorough. Got the job done quickly, without any fuss. Said that it wasn't a problem with *their* plumbing, either – something to do with the sewers, a council problem, something *they'd* have to fix. John hoped to

God that they'd do so quickly; he couldn't stand to see his toilet backed up like that again. It was disgusting. That poor bastard had needed to put his hand in it…

Oh well – that's what they paid him for.

John stood, naked except for his white Calvin Klein boxer shorts. He'd put on some weight recently, but his stomach was rounder now than it normally was, bloated by the excess of food being processed within. He scratched his belly, digging a finger into his belly button. He then pulled his bathrobe from the corner of the door, and swung it around his shoulders, tying a knot around his waist.

He crossed the landing quickly, the chill in the air causing his knees to shake. He was thankful that they'd decided to carpet the upstairs floors. Had the floors been laminate – just as Bev had wanted – then the wood underfoot right now would've been freezing. As it was, the carpet was far cosier and warm against the soles of his feet.

The floor of the bathroom would be a different matter, however.

They'd recently had the bathroom remodelled. It had cost them a small fortune, but John had to admit that it had been worth it. All the walls were panelled, making them much easier to clean. They'd had a double vanity unit fitted, so that they each had a basin of their own. This wasn't John's idea; Bev had wanted it. He didn't see the point – it wasn't as if they ever brushed their teeth at the same time anyway. But that's how marriages work; compromise – John got the carpet on the landing, Bev got the double vanity unit. Underfloor heating had been installed (oh, how John wished *that* were on right now), and the floor had been tiled with extremely expensive tiles.

Right now, those tiles felt as if they were made of ice.

John used the pull cord to switch on the bathroom light. The LEDs that had been installed were far brighter than the halogen bulbs that had been there before, and they burned into John's retinas. Shielding his eyes, he shut the door behind him and crossed the bathroom blind. That was fine; he'd navigated that room a million times before, so he didn't need to be able to see in order to find the toilet.

Once he was there, he used his free hand – the one *not* clamped over his eyes – to untie the knot in his robe and to pull down his underwear. And then he sat.

Keeping his eyes closed, he leaned forward, propping himself up, his hands on his chin, his elbows digging into his knees. He could quite easily have fallen asleep right there. In order to prevent himself from doing so, he tried to think about various things, such as how the white light of the LEDs looked purple through his eyelids, and how a linoleum floor would probably have been warmer, and how eating an entire naan bread to himself probably wasn't the wisest idea he'd ever had.

His stomach groaned as the waste matter inside him began to shift, his large intestine squirming like a slippery eel, a noose tightening around his colon. It was then that his first contraction came. Yep, this was almost certainly comparable to childbirth.

He sat there for what felt like an hour, a burning sensation growing in his bowels. He had to keep tensing every muscle in his body just to try and quell the ever-increasing pain.

Feces Of Death

This, most certainly, wasn't what he'd signed up for. Never again would he be ordering the vindaloo.

In actual fact, never again would he be ordering from that particular takeaway. For all he knew, it wasn't the curry itself that had caused this sudden and unexpected bout of severe indigestion/constipation – it was their shitty cooking and their complete disregard of food hygiene standards.

Regardless of all this, John still had work to do. He pushed, his sphincter eventually opening up to allow passage of what felt like a house brick.

Worse than childbirth, one hundred percent.

The pain was almost unbearable, but the relief he felt as the solid mass of fecal matter plopped into the water in the bottom of the bowl was almost orgasmic. John sat there for a few moments, breathing deeply, contemplating whether he ought to laugh or cry.

It was then that he felt something cold and wet swipe across the puckered opening of his rectum.

Quickly, he opened his eyes for the first time, his irises adjusting to accept the harsh light. The unexpected – and highly uncomfortable – sensation drew his eyes downward, between his thighs. He expected to see his ginormous turd there, so big that it protruded from the water, having collapsed under its own massive weight, and slumped against his arsehole.

But that's not what he saw.

At least, that's not the only thing he saw. There was something else there, something alive, something moving. It looked black and wet…

Of course it was wet! It was under the goddamn water!

That fucking rat!

It had to be the rat that he'd seen in there earlier, back when the toilet had been blocked. He *knew* he'd seen it then, and he knew for damn-sure he was seeing it now. It was there, squirming around in the bottom of the bowl, coiling itself around John's massive turd log.

John's brain processed all these thoughts in less than half a second. Still, that was too long for him to *really* process what it was he was seeing. He wasn't quick enough to recognise the danger he was in, not quick enough to stand from the toilet, to take himself out of harm's way.

The thing down in the toilet sprang forth from the water and entered John, squeezing itself into his anus.

John gasped, grasping onto the corner of the vanity unit beside him. A terrible burning sensation exploded from his rectum, as if he'd just been given a gasoline enema, and a lit match had been inserted into his sphincter. The thing in the toilet continued to fill his colon, expanding to the point that he could feel his internal tissues beginning to split. He could feel the warmth of his blood seeping out of him.

It was then that he found the ability to scream.

"John?" Bev's shrill and panic-stricken voice called from somewhere along the landing – or perhaps a million miles away. "JOHN?!"

John couldn't respond. There was something moving inside of him, something soft and malleable, reaching out of the toilet, out of the sewers, penetrating him, *violating* him, digging its teeth into his flesh.

Teeth?

What the *fuck*?

But that was what John felt. It was as if somebody had fed a length of barbed wire into him, and was twisting it, the pointed claws shredding his insides, ever-expanding, pushing outward, tearing through his bladder. His skin continued to split further, his scrotum ripping open, his mangled testes falling loose.

"John! John? What's going on?"

John was still screaming, blood spurting out from between his legs, coating his thighs, cascading down his shins, matting his leg hair. But John couldn't move, couldn't free himself from the grasp of the thing crawling inside of him.

Bev burst into the bathroom, her own gown wrapped around her body, just in time to see John's insides torn free from his body, and sucked down the toilet, his intestines slithering away like a clew of worms, blood and dirty water spilling out of the lavatory, flooding the tiled floor.

She was screaming then, too.

John stood from the toilet. Everything between his legs was missing. A gaping hole now existed between his thighs, a cavernous void bored through his groin, much of his chest cavity having been hollowed out. He stumbled forward, his ankles bound together by his boxer shorts, then collapsed to the floor, dying face down in a puddle of gore.

CHAPTER EIGHT
A Woman's Work Is Never Done

Martin had set his alarm for 6:00 a.m. To him, this constituted a lie-in. As such, Emily had set her own alarm for 5:30. She wasn't really an early riser – never had been – and today was her day off, but she wanted to get up early, so that she could make Martin breakfast in bed. As soon as the alarm started beeping, she grabbed her phone and shut it off, so as not to wake him.

Thankfully, he didn't even stir. Must've been the wine they'd drank last night.

Blindly snatching up one of Martin's oversized t-shirts, she climbed tentatively out of the bed, and pulled it on over her head. She was a petite girl, so the shirt almost reached to her knees. She looked herself over in the mirror, only to find that the t-shirt she was now wearing featured the grotesque image of two rotting cadavers seemingly pleasuring each other, the words '*Cannibal Corpse*' dripping with blood. Still, it hugged what little she had in the way of curves nicely. It'd have to do for now.

Quietly, Emily made her way downstairs and into the kitchen. She set the kettle to boil, then went about frying two sausages and an egg. Once they were cooked, she assembled them into a sandwich. With the kettle boiled, she made a mug of tea, then carried both back upstairs, and into the bedroom.

"Wakey, wakey, sleepy head," she said as she perched herself on the edge of the mattress. She placed the mug onto the bedside table, keeping a hold of the plate on which the sandwich sat.

"Huh?" said Martin, looking at her through squinted eyes. "What time is it?"

"Time for breakfast."

Martin smiled, pushing himself up onto his elbows. He blinked his eyes rapidly, regaining his vision. "Is that *my* t-shirt?"

"Oh, yeah," laughed Emily. She sat the plate down on the bed and turned, sitting up on her knees. "It was the closest thing to hand. You think it suits me?" She ran her hands over her body, smoothing the material out, intentionally pulling it tight against her breasts.

Martin raised his eyebrows, biting his lip. "It looks better on you than it does on me."

"You think?"

Martin nodded. Smiling, he sat up and wrapped his arm around Emily's waist, dragging her forward so that she now straddled him. Sliding his hands upward, beneath the material, he allowed his fingertips to trace a path along her spine. Emily bent, both hands on Martin's face. She kissed him, allowing it to linger. She loved Martin, more than anything.

Martin lifted the t-shirt up and over Emily's head, tossing it to one side. Naked now, she kissed him again. Martin pulled her down on top of him, then rolled to the side, forcing her to her back and shifting his weight on top of her. Emily loved the feeling of Martin on top of her; the warmth of his body somehow made her feel safe.

Pleasure ran through her body as Martin shifted downward, placing a delicate kiss on every inch of her skin. He kissed her neck and her collarbone. He kissed between her breasts, then kissed each of her stiffening nipples. He kissed all the way down to her navel. He kissed the inside of her thighs.

Emily giggled, the sensation of Martin's stubble tickling her legs. "Stop," she moaned, half-heartedly, knowing full-well that Martin *wouldn't* stop, and finding herself entirely glad of this fact.

She grasped the bedsheets, screwing them tightly in her fists, as the feeling of ecstasy began to course through her body.

***

Martin didn't leave the house until some time after 7:30.

His phone was ringing before he even made it to his van. As expected, it was David. Martin answered the call. "Good morning," he said.

"Where are you?" asked David, his voice almost sounding frantic, any chance of exchanging pleasantries gone out the window. He sounded exhausted; Martin wondered if he'd even gotten any sleep last night.

Feces Of Death

"I've just left the house," Martin replied, fishing his keys from his jacket pocket, pressing the button on the fob to open the back doors. There, he loaded his toolbox into the back of the van. "Just heading into the office now. Why? What's up?"

"This is a fucking joke, that's what's up."

David didn't sound happy at all, and Martin couldn't help but feel somewhat amused by this. "What is a joke?" he asked, stifling his own laughter.

"It's been non-stop all night. You wanna know how many voicemails I found on the answering machine this morning? I'll tell you, shall I? Fifty-fucking-seven! Fifty-seven! It's fucking ridiculous."

Fifty-seven *was* ridiculous, Martin had to agree. How could so many people have so many issues with their plumbing, all at the same time? It had to be something to do with the issue in the sewers — assuming there was some sort of an issue. There had to be, right? These sorts of problems didn't just materialise out of nothing; there had to be something in the sewers, causing the wastewater to back up in the way that it was. "Have you spoken to the guys at the processing plant?" he asked.

"I've tried," said David. "I've called them three times already. Nobody's answering."

"Great. Very helpful."

"Don't bother coming into the office," David continued. "I need you to head on over to Holloway Lane. There's three houses on that street that have blockages that need fixing. I can't give you any more details than that. Just get over there and see what you can do. Let me know if there's any problems."

"Three blockages? All on the same street? How is that even possible?"

"You tell me…"

Martin shook his head, more for his own benefit than for the benefit of anybody else. "Okay," he said, climbing into the driver's seat of the van. "I'm on my way there right now. I'll let you know if I find anything that might help solve this problem."

"Well, I won't hold my breath. But, thanks - I'll keep trying the plant. They *have to* know something by now!"

"Yeah. You'd have thought so."

"Sorry about this, Martin," David said, sounding entirely empathetic now. "But it looks like it's gonna be a busy day today."

Martin sighed. He pushed the key into the ignition and fired up the engine. "Yep. Looks like it."

***

Emily spent most of the morning pottering around the house. Being her day off, she did consider the possibility of just relaxing for the day. Perhaps she might even take a nap. But then she decided against it. It wasn't like her to sit around doing nothing; she always liked to be busy.

The sex she'd had – both last night and this morning – had left her feeling satisfied, reinvigorated and highly energetic. It had been just what she'd needed.

She tidied the kitchen, rearranging the two-dozen mugs they'd somehow managed to accumulate, into what she considered to be a more sensible order. Many of them went unused nowadays anyway, but instead of throwing them out, she decided to shift those particular mugs to the back of the cupboard.

Feces Of Death

She vacuumed downstairs. She polished the fireplace. She changed the bedsheets.

For lunch, she made herself a ham-salad sandwich, which she ate on the sofa while watching her favourite daytime chat show.

After lunch, she decided to clean the bathroom. It was possibly her least favourite job around the house, but Martin was never likely to do it, and even if he did, he wouldn't do it properly. Emily loved him wholeheartedly, but when it came to housework, he was completely useless. If anything needed fixing, he was the perfect man for the job. Want something cleaned? Forget about it. Martin made most of the mess in the house, and whenever she'd asked him to tidy up, he always managed to somehow make things worse.

Well, a woman's work is never done.

Emily took down the shower head and scrubbed away the limescale that had accumulated there. She used a soft cloth to wipe away the watermarks that grubbied the chrome fittings. She then replaced the shower head and moved on to the toilet.

Pretty much everything in the bathroom needed to be cleaned with mild soapy water. Pretty much everything was susceptible to chemical damage. Except for the toilet. The vanity unit that enclosed the cistern couldn't get bleach on it, but the toilet bowl itself was perfectly safe. Emily wiped over the toilet seat with her soapy cloth, and then squirted a thick trail of bleach under the rim, watching as it slowly trickled its way down into the water. She watched it for a few minutes, almost mesmerised by the way it slowly cascaded down the porcelain.

Once she felt that the bleach had had enough time to do its thing, she flushed.

The water in the bottom of the bowl *gurgled*, but it didn't go anywhere. The new water entering the bowl washed the diluted bleach down the smooth surface, but then only began to fill the bowl. "Oh, shit," Emily muttered to herself.

With the water now precariously close to overflowing, Emily knew she shouldn't flush again. Staring at the water, she tried to consider all her options.

But then a slurp came from the water, a sucking noise, like a hungry fish chomping at the surface of a lake, stealing the bread that had been thrown for the ducks. The water squelched, then disappeared, washed away into the sewers hidden deep beneath the house.

Relieved, Emily stood. She retrieved her phone from the back pocket of her jeans and dialled Martin.

It took a few rings – he was busy, no doubt – but eventually he answered. "Hey," said Emily, trying to sound as cheery as possible. "How's it going?"

"Well," said Martin, sounding almost exasperated, as if he were about to deliver a laundry list of problems and issues he'd already had to deal with so far today. Thankfully, he kept it brief. "So far, in the space of the last three hours, I've had to unblock eight shit-filled toilets."

"Well," said Emily, not really sure she wanted to be the bearer of bad news. "Don't shoot the messenger, but I'm afraid to tell you - I think our toilet is blocked too."

"You're fucking kidding me…"

Feces Of Death

"Sorry. Is there anything I can do to try and fix it?"

"No. I need to take a look at it myself, really. Just don't flush it, otherwise you'll end up making a mess everywhere."

"You got it. Okay, well - I'll see you later, okay?"

"Alright. Have a good day."

"You too. Bye." Emily hung up the phone. She looked down into the toilet, watching as bubbles filtered up, out of the u-bend, bursting on the shimmering surface of the toilet water.

CHAPTER NINE
Two Weeks' Notice

Andy had had enough. He was too good for this place. He'd joined the company hoping to make some kind of a difference to the way they worked. Fresh out of university, he believed that he might be able to offer something to this company that they'd never seen before. Bring something new to the table, so to speak. But they weren't interested. Instead, they had him plodding along, day by day, putting out the same old crap they'd always done.

Where was the excitement? Where was the innovation?

Everything this company did was boring. The people were boring. The job was boring. Andy knew for certain – he felt it in his bones – that a better opportunity was out there waiting for him, just beyond the boundaries of this good-for-nothing company.

That was why he'd decided to hand in his resignation.

Next week.

He'd do it next week…

Feces Of Death

Andy worked as a designer for an engineering company. They manufactured enclosures for electrical installations, both from steel and from plastic. There wasn't much design work to be done, as there wasn't much new to add to these things. No point in reinventing the wheel, you know? But still, Andy had assumed that there would be something to sink his teeth into. As it so happened, all he was expected to do was draw up all the original designs, and make alterations when it was discovered that certain elements didn't actually work as expected, despite having been out in the hands of consumers for months (even years, sometimes).

It was fine. It paid the bills. But Andy wanted more; more responsibility, more money.

So, yes – he was definitely leaving.

Sooner, rather than later.

Andy made his way along the corridor and down the stairs, down to the ground floor. This was where the only working toilets in the building were situated. The upstairs toilets had been out of order for some time now, as *somebody* had, for reasons unknown, taken to flushing bundles of paper towels down there.

Andy made his way along the downstairs corridor. As he neared the corner, Louise and Dawn emerged from the sales office just a few feet ahead.

Dawn was an older lady, and was secretary to the sales manager. Louise was around Andy's age. She carried a little excess weight, but she had long blonde hair which she wore perfectly straight between her shoulder blades, and a perfect smile, with perfectly straight teeth, so Andy was willing to look past her slight obesity. Besides, her tits were huge; Andy had on many occasions imagined what his dick might look like sandwiched between them.

He wished he could talk to her. He wished he could say something funny, to get her to laugh, to get her to even notice him. He'd love nothing more than to get to know her better, and to take her out on a date. Fucking her would be the ultimate goal, of course, but a nice meal and a bottle of wine beforehand wouldn't go amiss. But Andy was too shy, too cowardly to say anything. She'd probably laugh at *him*, not his joke. She'd reject him, and make him feel about two feet tall.

So, instead, he waved and offered a smile, just like he always did. Louise and Dawn reciprocated, like always, then continued on, along the corridor, and into the ladies bathroom.

When Andy entered the men's toilet, he found that both urinals were already occupied; Stan from accounts was standing before one, while that arsehole Carl from planning was standing before the other. Neither of them acknowledged Andy as he entered, and that was fine.

There were three cubicles in the bathroom, all of which were empty. Andy only needed to piss, and he hated it when people used the cubicles for this purpose – what were they scared of? Did they think people were going to try and look at their cock? But with the urinals taken, what other choice did he have?

He entered the first cubicle and closed the door behind him, sliding the lock into place. He unzipped his trousers, pulled out his penis, and began to urinate. The two men from the urinals left almost immediately after, making him wish he'd waited for just a minute, instead of his now looking like one of those people he despised so much, scared of those imagined perverts who so desired to ogle them.

As the urine leaked from him, offering him sweet relief, he took his phone from his pocket and unlocked it. It crossed his mind to open up the JobSeeker app, to see if there was anything that piqued his interest. He'd so far spent a total of around twenty minutes on the app, looking at what jobs were available. He was definitely leaving this job, definitely handing on his notice next week. He'd put more effort into finding another job after then. He'd have to.

Because he was *definitely* quitting next week.

Or the week after that, maybe, at the very latest.

So instead of JobSeeker, he opened Twitter, and scrolled through the feed, finding that nobody had posted anything of interest.

Right then, somehow – God knows how it *actually* happened – but Andy dropped his phone…

It almost seemed as if it happened in slow motion. Perhaps it was because he was scrolling with his left, weaker hand, his right wrapped around his cock, directing the stream of piss into the bowl. Whatever it was that caused it, Andy watched in horror as the phone flipped a half dozen times, bounced from the rim of the lavatory, then tumbled into the water, his own piss splashing from the screen. "Oh, fuck me!" he grunted, cursing his own bad luck. He literally couldn't believe it.

And then he found himself feeling grateful – grateful for the fact that those two dickheads had left the toilet a few minutes earlier, and hadn't been there to witness his misfortune.

For fuck's sake. It was this *fucking* place. Not only was it a shitty place to work, but it was also bad luck.

The phone would be fine; it was high end, and was fully waterproof. But that didn't take away from the fact that he'd pissed all over it. He wouldn't be telling anybody about this. No fucking way.

With no choice in the matter, Andy dropped to his knees and reached into the bowl, his fingers slipping from the smooth glass of his phone, as he tried to fish it out of the piss-infused water. It slipped once, but then he managed to grasp it.

Then something grasped *him*.

Something latched onto his arm, coiled around his wrist, squeezing it like a boa constrictor. Something in the toilet.

What in the name of Jesus fucking Christ?

Andy tried to pull against it, but whatever it was, it was too strong. It held him tightly, dragging him downward, as if it were trying to pull him into the toilet. And then there was a pain, something sharp digging into his skin, clamping down onto the bone, what he imagined it might feel like to be bitten by an alligator. An incredible pain shot through his body as his skin began to tear.

He screamed.

Andy pulled and pulled, a searing wave of torment raking through his nerves every time he did so. He looked down to the toilet bowl filling with blood – filling with *his* blood. As he tried to wrench his arm free, writhing as his arm was sucked further and further into the pipes, the water and blood splashed in torrents, pouring over the rim of the toilet, flooding the tiled bathroom floor.

Whatever those sharp things were, there were more of them now, tearing through his skin like fishhooks, peeling his flesh from the bone.

Something finally gave. Andy's hand pulled free. He stumbled backward, colliding with the flimsy cubicle door. He watched, terror infiltrating every inch of his body, as a bundle of shredded meat, like torn rags, soaked in gore, disappeared down the toilet. He lifted his hand, his eyes growing wide as they fell on all that remained.

He could see his bones, slathered in ichor. All the flesh had been stripped away, leaving only savaged ligaments to hold the metatarsal bones in place. There was no skin, no muscle left. The bones sagged and knocked together uncontrollably. The meat sat ragged around radius and ulna bone, the raw flesh seeping gore, splattering it onto his shirt, staining the white cotton a deep crimson, plastering it onto his skin.

Andy fumbled the lock and pulled the door open, staggering sideways into the flimsy chipboard wall of the cubicle. He slumped forward, blood gushing from the haggard remains of his arm, splashing in the sinks, and spraying over the mirror.

He collapsed to the floor, too weak to run, too weak to escape this godforsaken place, too weak to find himself help.

He knew he should've quit this job. He should've done it last week.

He died there on the bathroom floor, his blood blooming into a gigantic puddle around him.

In the toilet, his phone was ringing, the incessant tone muffled by the blood-and-piss-infused water in which it sat.

CHAPTER TEN
The Men In Suits

Martin's phone was ringing once again. He pulled it from his pocket, already knowing that it was going to be David.

He checked the time displayed in the top corner of the screen. It was 16:27. He was due to finish in three minute's time, but that seemed increasingly unlikely. For starters, he couldn't very well leave his current job in the half-finished state it was in. It wouldn't look all too professional, were he to down tools and walk out of there at four-thirty on the dot, leaving the customer with a toilet full of shitty water and a bath that wouldn't drain. No. At the very least, he'd have to leave them with a functional toilet.

But then, Martin already knew that this wouldn't be his last job of the day. If David was phoning him now, it could only be to give him more work.

"Hello?" said Martin, as he answered the call.

"Martin," said David, once again forgoing any pleasantries. "Are you still on Felton Drive?"

"I am, yes."

"Great! I need you to do me a favour - there's a team working on the next street along. They're putting a camera down the drains, to see if they can find anything. Can you go over there, and check in on them? Let me know if they find anything?"

"Sure. I mean - I *am* in the middle of something right now, so I just need to finish…"

"No, no, no, no, no," said David, an urgent tone to his voice. "I need you out there now. I'll send Steve over to pick up your job."

"Why don't you get Steve to check on the camera team?"

"Are you serious?" snorted David. "You think I'd trust *him* to actually find out what's going on? Not a chance in hell. If I asked him to go over there, he probably wouldn't even bother. He'd just sit in his van, then tell me they didn't find anything. No, this is far too important. I need *you* to go for me."

Andy couldn't help but feel some sense of pride. Such high praise wasn't often lavished onto him, certainly not from David. The two of them had been good friends once, but they'd drifted apart since David had taken the management job. Martin had somewhat resented him for it at first, but now he realised he was much better off where he was. "Okay," he said. "I'll head out there right now. When will Steve get here?"

"He said he's five minutes away."

"Okay. I'll let you know what we find."

The customer hadn't been too impressed when Martin had said he needed to leave. But he informed them that his colleague would be there momentarily, and that he himself would return in an hour or so, to check that their problem had been fixed.

Martin found the team working at the junction between the two streets. There were three of them, all men, all looking like they'd rather be at home sticking needles into their respective scrotums, than having to be there. One of the men was on his knees, perched on the edge of an open manhole cover. The other two men were standing a few feet away, watching a video monitor. As Martin approached, he saw that the man on his knees was holding the handle of some sort of device, directing it into the sewer. He understood then that this was the camera, and the man was operating it, driving it through the pipes. The other two men were watching the video being fed by the camera.

"That's it," said one of the men watching the monitor. "Just keep taking it forward. Nice and steady now."

"This is bullshit," said the camera operator. "What do they think we're gonna find? Something big enough to block an entire street ain't gonna be in any of these pipes, is it?"

"But it isn't the entire street," said the other observer. "That's the point. It's only a few clusters of houses. And the fact is, it still looks as if it's moving."

"That's not possible."

"I know. And that's why we're here - to find out what's *actually* going on."

The man on his knees shook his head and scoffed. "I still think it's bullshit."

Martin approached from behind, moving slowly so as to hear as much of their conversation as he could. What did he mean, the blockage was *moving*? Was such a thing even possible? He'd imagined some huge fatberg, clogging the sewer pipes; such a thing couldn't move anywhere. But then, these men had to be looking for *something*. Martin wondered who exactly had sent them.

"Excuse me," Martin said, as he drew near. "I work for EcoPlumb. My boss just asked me to come on over here and see if you guys had found anything."

All three of the men looked at Martin, with an incredulous look about them. They then went on with their work. For a moment, Martin expected them to ignore him completely, to act as if he wasn't even there. But then one of the men spoke. "No," he said, bluntly. "We don't know anything just yet."

"Do you mind if I hang around? See what you do find?"

"Be my guest. But, if I'm being totally honest with you, I imagine you'll be wasting your time. I don't think we're gonna find anything here."

Martin said nothing more, just moved in a little closer, stepping between the two men and peering over their shoulders. The image in the monitor was blurry, static buzzing over the picture. It was dark, the light that was no doubt attached to the front of the camera illuminating little more than a small circle, just a few inches ahead. The inside of the pipes were encrusted with filth. The shit that adhered to the inner walls glistened.

And then, on the screen, the camera hit into something, the entire image turning black. The operator grunted as his efforts were halted.

"Hold up," said one of the observers. "There's something there. Back up a little, would you?"

Groaning, the operator wound the camera backwards. The image on the monitor shifted, then cleared. It seemed to show some sort of solid mass filling the full diameter of the pipe. This mass, whatever it was, was a blackish-brown in colour, and looked as if it might be malleable, despite having so far held firm.

"Is that shit?" said one of the men, mirroring the thought that had just popped into Martin's head.

The other man shook his head and shrugged his shoulders simultaneously.

"If it *is* shit," said Martin. "Then surely there must be something behind it, preventing it from moving. Feces won't just get stuck like that, not in multiple pipes, affecting so many homes."

All three of the men looked at Martin once again. It was clear that they didn't want *his* input. None of them had asked for *his* opinion. Again, without saying a word, they went back about their business. But then, again, the man who had spoken to Martin before, spoke once again. "No," he said. "You're right. We need to see if we can get past this blockage, find out what's behind it."

"So, what then?" growled the man on his knees, his frustration growing.

"Let's see if we can slide past it. Perhaps move the camera right across to the side - any side - and then push forward, see if we can create a gap."

"Alright."

On the screen, Martin watched as the picture from the camera shifted all the way to the right, then forward. It pushed into the side of the brown mass, peeling it partly away from the wall of the pipes.

And then it moved.

Did it move?

Martin was sure the mass had moved. Whatever the hell it was, it seemed to contract like a muscle, sucking itself in, the light shimmering from its undulating body. Was it an animal? Was it some sort of living organism?

It hadn't moved far, just shifted a little, moving an inch or so along the pipe. But the other men had seen it too. Evidently, the camera operator had *felt* it move. "What the fuck was that?" he said. "Is there something down there? I swear to God, something just tugged on the camera."

"Back up a bit," said one of the men. The operator did as instructed. The image on screen showed the same mass, only now it seemed to be adhered to just one side of the pipe. The other side seemed to be open. "Did we dislodge part of it?"

"Maybe," said the other man. Then to the camera operator – "Move across to the right, then forwards. We may be able to get past now."

The on-screen picture shifted across, then past the blockage. It seemed that whatever it was stretched endlessly along the entire length of the pipe. Martin may have considered the fact that this was something that had settled there, before solidifying – he'd seen similar things before, especially with fats and soaps. But this hadn't settled here. It couldn't have; it was on the *top* of the pipe.

The excrement – if that's what this was – moved again. It was like a pulse; a brief swelling that travelled along the length like a wave.

"What the…" muttered one of the men.

And then the mass began to slide along the tube, slithering along like a snake in a tunnel, sliding from side to side, looping around the pipe, top to bottom.

"What the fuck?" exclaimed the camera operator. Martin looked to see that his arms were shaking, the handle of the device rattling in his hands.

On the screen, the mass swelled, filling the pipe once more, filling the entire image with black.

The camera operator was yanked forward, knocking him off his feet, sending him sprawling onto his belly. The handle of the camera pulled free from his grip, and disappeared down the manhole. "Holy shit!"

The image from the camera fuzzed, pixelated distortion filling the image. And then it was black, the signal lost.

The four men standing over the open manhole looked silently at each other. It seemed clear to Martin that none of them understood what had just happened. But what Martin did know was that, whatever that thing was down there, it *had* been alive.

Was it that which had caused the blockage?

The ringing of Martin's phone was the first thing to break the silence. He pulled it from his pocket. It was David. Martin answered the call. "David," he said. "You're never gonna believe this."

"No," said David, his high-pitched voice sounding all the more frantic. "*You're* not going to believe *this*. I need you to get back here right away. There are some people here. I need you to hear what they've got to say."

***

As Martin drove to the office, he couldn't help but think about what he'd just witnessed, that thing in the pipes. Had it *really* been alive? It had looked soft and slimy. Not like a snake – more like an eel. He'd seen it move, he was sure of it. Seen it with his own two eyes. Was that even possible? *Something* had pulled the camera into the sewers. It had to be something they hadn't seen, something hidden behind the excrement, out of sight of the camera.

It was almost dark by the time Martin arrived at the EcoPlumb office. It had gone 18:00, and dusk had settled quickly, the orange sun setting beyond the horizon, as Martin had raced along the highway.

The office was situated within a small industrial area, accessed via the forecourt of a garage. Martin navigated through the petrol pumps and through a narrow opening, into the industrial units.

All of the other units had closed by now, the businesses that occupied them having shut for the evening. But the lights inside the EcoPlumb office were still on.

Outside the office, there were four black cars parked sporadically throughout the parking area. They were all black, with blacked out windows, and shiny, chrome wheels. At the front door of the office were two men. Both wore suits. Both stood tall, their hands behind their backs. They looked as if they meant business.

Martin parked up and climbed out of his van. "What the hell is going on?" he asked, as he approached the door, and, therefore, the two men.

One of the men stepped forward, his hand outstretched before him. The light touch of his fingers on Martin's chest was enough to force him to stop. "Are you Martin?" the man asked.

"Yes. I am. And who the fuck are you?"

The besuited man didn't offer an answer. Instead, he said – "Come on. They're waiting for you." He then directed Martin into the building, that same hand pressed delicately against his back.

Martin felt as if he were in trouble. He felt as if he were being arrested, as if this guy were leading him into an interrogation room (although Martin was certain that no such thing existed within the EcoPlumb offices), ready to shine a light in his eyes, and break his fingers to extract the information he wanted. Martin's heart was racing. It wasn't until he was led into David's office that he felt *slightly* more comfortable.

David was perched on the edge of his desk. There were four other men in the room with him, all dressed in suits, much like the men who had apparently been waiting for *him* outside.

"Jesus, Martin!" said David, the moment his eyes fell on Martin. He stood from the desk and marched across the room, slapping him across the shoulders. "Thank God you're here. This is fucking insane. You're never gonna believe this." He was speaking at a million miles an hour, each successive word blending with the last. "I've never heard anything like it in my life. It's impossible. That's it - it's impossible. I think these people are crazy. But - holy shit - if any of this is real, then we're all fucked!"

Martin's brain was fuzzy, struggling to assemble all the thoughts that were ricocheting inside his skull. "What's going on?" he looked from David to the other men in the room.

One of the men stepped forward. "Martin," he offered a hand, which Martin promptly shook. "My name is Bill Harper. I represent PharmaCom."

"The pharmaceutical company?" Martin asked.

"That's correct. Me and my team have been sent here to look into an *incident* that may have occurred here a few weeks ago."

Martin shook head. "What incident? And what's that got to do with us? Is this something to do with the blockages?" Again, he was looking between David, Bill, and the other men, to whom he had yet to be introduced.

"Possibly," sighed Bill, exasperated. "We at PharmaCom are always working to come up with new innovations - ways for us to help heal the sick, to bring comfort to those in pain, to extend life. To revitalise and rejuvenate. Our latest product was in the final stages of development, and, as such, a quantity needed to be sent from our northern facility to our southern facility…"

"That's just outside of town, right?" Martin interjected.

"That is correct. It's this facility where the majority of our testing takes place."

Martin listened, unsure of what any of this had to do with him. The man – Bill – was well spoken. The suit seemed to fit him well, like he was made for this role (whatever the hell his role actually was).

"As everything we do at PharmaCom needs to remain top secret, it was decided that it would be in the company's best interest to make this an overnight delivery, and, in order to protect our anonymity further, we chose to use a relatively small, and therefore unknown haulage company to transport the chemical for us. This, you see, was our biggest error. As it so happened, they were highly unprofessional, to say the least. We can't be certain of all the details, but they somehow managed to lose a barrel of the chemical. We have since located this barrel, sitting in the bed of a stream, just a mile outside of this very town. Unfortunately, the barrel had split open, and some of the chemical managed to find its way into the sewer system."

Martin could feel himself frowning. "So, something you spilled into our sewers is causing the blockages? I mean… How is that possible?"

David snorted a laugh, shaking his head in disbelief. "Wait 'til you hear *this*," he said.

Bill rolled his eyes. He then continued. "Until today, we didn't know exactly *what* we were dealing with. Ever since we discovered the missing barrel, we've been conducting surveillance on all communications in and out of town. As such, we know all about the numerous blockages you've been dealing with over the past few days. In the early hours of this morning, we received reports of a man having been attacked by something that apparently emerged from his toilet."

"Attacked? By what?"

"We don't know for sure."

"Didn't the man *say* what it was?"

Slowly, Bill shook his head. "He couldn't. Whatever it was, it killed him. It tore his insides out."

Martin felt the blood drain from his face. His brain felt numb. He couldn't quite wrap his head around what he was being told. "Are we…" he mumbled, trying to assemble the jigsaw of thoughts rattling around in his mind. "Is this some sort of animal?"

"We believe," Bill continued. "Whatever it was that killed this man… Well… We believe that we are responsible for its existence. You see, the chemical that was spilled was actually capable of reinvigorating dead cells. It was designed to be used in an anti-aging cream. However, in such a concentrated form - as it was inside that barrel - it actually has the ability to entirely resurrect dead cells, essentially bringing them back to life. As such, we don't believe we're dealing with a natural predator here."

"A *natural* predator? I'm sorry, but I don't think I understand what you're trying to tell me."

"When we - as people - when we eat, we digest millions of different living organisms. As they pass through our digestive system, everything becomes sort of intertwined. All the DNA gets mashed up into one big, jumbled mess. That's why the police can't use DNA taken from feces as evidence in court - there's no telling what's really in there."

Martin shook his head for what felt like the millionth time. He could feel his annoyance beginning to escalate. "What are you getting at?"

"Our chemical may have resurrected that jumble of cells, into some sort of creature... not of this world. Some sort of hybrid animal, constructed from all the DNA our substance came into contact with. Essentially, a creature made up of all the waste matter floating around in your sewers."

Martin rubbed his palm across his forehead. "A monster?" he said.

The men looked at one another. None of them answered.

"A monster made of shit?" said Martin.

Still no response.

"And you think this monster is somehow causing these blockages?"

"We don't actually know what's causing the blockages. All we know is, there is a creature... Or perhaps, *multiple* creatures hiding in the sewers below this town, and they have started to kill people."

"So what the *fuck* do you intend to do about it?" said Martin, his anger boiling over.

"We need to start by locating it... or them," said Bill. "The man who died, he was one of your customers - you fixed his blockage just yesterday."

Suddenly, a realisation hit Martin. And then fear began to swell in his chest, as if his heart were on fire. "Wait," he said, his hands raised in surrender. "The blockage in his house, could it have been caused by one of these monsters trying to get out?"

"Perhaps," said Bill, shrugging his shoulders.

Martin looked to David. "Emily called me earlier. She said that our toilet was blocked at home."

A sense of panic filled the room. The men in suits seemed to be communicating telepathically, all thinking the exact same thought. Bill placed a hand on Martin's shoulder. "And where, exactly, do you live?"

"Hawthorne Avenue," Martin said. "On the other side of town. I need to get back there now."

"We'll come with you."

"Sir," said one of the other besuited men, interrupting Bill. He was flicking his index finger over the screen of his iPad. "I think you need to look at this."

Bill stormed over to him, and snatched the iPad from his hands. "Oh shit," he muttered, somewhat under his breath.

Martin's heart was in his throat. "What is it?"

"Somebody else has been attacked. A man has had his arm ripped off, over on Lakeshore Industrial Estate. We need to get over there right now!"

"What about my place?" asked Martin.

"Sorry, but we know for certain that something happened here. We don't even know what's happening at your house." Bill then motioned to the other men with a wave of his hand. "Move out, and get yourselves armed up. We need to find these fuckers quickly, and nip this whole fuckin' thing in the bud."

The men were marching out of the office then, back into their black cars.

"Hey!" called Martin, chasing after them. "What about me? What about my girlfriend?"

"Sorry," Bill said once again. "If you find anything, let us know. But *this* needs to be our priority."

The cars were gone then, each one blazing out of the car park and racing off along the road, disappearing into the darkness of the night.

David took Martin by the arm. "Come on," he said, urgency in his voice. "Let's go check that Emily is okay."

Martin nodded, grateful that David was still there with him.

CHAPTER ELEVEN
They Emerge

It had been a long day.

Every day was a long fucking day. Richard didn't love his job. He was well paid, but that didn't exactly make up for the tedium he felt day to day. As a special projects manager for a security installations company, he spent most of every day talking to idiot buyers about how good *his* company's systems were, and why they absolutely should not buy from their competitors.

It was fine. It paid the bills. But it wasn't *exciting*. As such, Richard had to find excitement elsewhere.

Every Friday, after work, before he'd head home to his wife, he'd stop by Olivia's place for a massage. And not just any old massage; a full service, body-to-body massage.

Richard loved his wife, of course. He and Judy had been married for nearly twenty years. But they were both in their late forties now, and Judy's libido had seemingly dried up and vanished into the ether. Richard, on the other hand, still needed sex; he was a

Feces Of Death

red-blooded male after all – it was only natural for him to feel the desire to sow his wild oats. But, despite the lack of sex, he and Judy got on wonderfully. He'd never leave her. It was much better for him to seek sexual satisfaction elsewhere.

And, the way he saw it, the fact that he was *paying* for it made this just a simple business transaction. There was no love involved here. That meant that this wasn't adulterous – he was simply procuring a service.

As always, he'd called ahead, and, as always, Olivia had already saved a slot for him. The usual time – six p.m.

When Olivia answered the door to her apartment, she did so with her body hidden behind it. This was the usual tactic of working girls, hiding themselves behind the door, just in case the person they answered it to *wasn't* the client they were expecting. And Richard didn't mind so much; the teasing only served to further turn him on.

"Hello, my sexy man," said Oliva, her thick Romanian accent muddying her words as always. She waved her hand, ushering Richard inside. "Come in, please."

Richard didn't need to be asked twice.

Inside, with the door closed, Olivia pressed her soft, plump lips to Richard's own, allowing her tongue to slide into his mouth, knowing that this was something he enjoyed immensely. When they separated, Richard took a step back and looked Olivia over. She was perfect. She was only twenty-four. She had long, brunette hair. Her skin was perfectly tanned. She was tall and slender, her firm abdominal muscles visible under the soft skin of her stomach. She was wearing black lingerie, the bra barely big enough to retain her surgically enhanced breasts. A silk robe hung lazily over her shoulders.

"So," smiled Olivia, ever the seductress. "Should we get the paperwork out of the way, so we can begin?"

"Of course." Richard pulled an envelope from the inside pocket of his jacket, Olivia's fee nestled safely inside. He handed it over.

Olivia flicked her thumb over the notes inside, counting it quickly. Satisfied, she stashed the envelope into a drawer, then took Richard by the hand. "You look like you've had a hard day," she whispered into his ear. "Perhaps you might like to take a shower."

"Indeed," smirked Richard. "I think a shower might be in order."

Olivia led Richard through the living room, into the bathroom. There, she helped him out of his jacket, before pulling his tie loose and slipping it off over his head. She then turned her back to him. "Would you mind?" she said, sultry.

Richard knew exactly what this meant. "Of course," he said, as he unfastened her bra, allowing his fingers to slide across the silky skin of her back.

As she slipped the lacey garment from her shoulders, she turned to face Richard once more. Richard stared in awe at her perfectly round breasts. They never ceased to amaze him. He slid his hands over them, cupping them, caressing them, allowing his palms to gently rub over her delicate nipples. His fingers ran below Olivia's breasts, tracing the scars where the implants had been inserted.

Olivia then helped Richard out of the rest of his clothes, before slipping off her own panties.

Naked now, Richard pulled Olivia in close, kissing her once more. Her hand found its way to his rock-hard erection. She stroked him back and forth, the pleasure surging through Richard's body almost enough to buckle his knees.

The shower was mounted over the bath, a glass screen separating it from the rest of the room. Olivia stepped into the bath, her hand remaining wrapped tightly around Richard's throbbing cock. Richard followed her in.

Olivia turned the knob on the wall, to turn on the shower. A clunking-clang reverberated through the pipes as the water seemed to struggle through – trapped air restricting its movement, no doubt. But then the water flowed, already warm as it cascaded down Richard's body.

Olivia instructed him to turn, to place his hands on the wall. Richard did so. Olivia then began to massage a handful of shower gel into his back and shoulders, the lather washing over his body, the scent of lavender filling the room. She reached around to his front, caressing his chest. A decade ago, Richard had been quite muscular, his chest and abs quite firm. But over the past few years, as age had started to take its toll on his body, he had become lazy. Now his body was soft, a ring of flab beginning to form around his midsection. But Olivia never seemed to mind; certainly, she never commented. Instead, she allowed her hands to wander down between his legs once again, the lubrication of the shower gel increasing the ecstasy tenfold.

Richard turned, breaking Olivia's grip on his member before she made him cum too soon. They kissed again, Richard reaching around her body, caressing her back, groping at her buttocks.

More popping and clunking came from the pipes. The water spurted from the shower head once more, the flow interrupted sporadically. "I think you need to get a plumber in," laughed Richard.

"Yes," agreed Olivia. "This start happen only today. I call them later. But do not worry about this now, baby. Now, I must see to *your* needs."

Her hands were on his cock once again. Olivia pushed Richard so that his back was against the wall. She then squatted down and took him in her mouth.

Richard ran his fingers through Olivia's saturated hair, guiding her head as she bobbed up and down along the length of his erection, expertly sucking it down into her throat, not even gagging in the slightest. Richard tipped his head back and closed his eyes. The water from the shower splashed over his face, filling his mouth.

But there was something else there, other than the water. A distinct taste on his tongue. Something vile, disgusting.

And that smell…

Richard opened his eyes to see that the water now flowing from the shower was dirty. And not only was it dirty; it was thick and brown, sputtering out of the tiny holes in the shower head, spattering his entire body with feces. "Oh, what the *fuck*!" he groaned, his sudden movement knocking Olivia onto her backside.

The black-ish sludge slopped over his body, coating his skin. It felt strange, as if it were tugging at his hairs. And then it was burning him. It was cold – he was certain of that much – but still the pain he felt was like he was bathing in scalding hot water. It was as if it were dissolving his flesh, melting it from his bones.

And Olivia was under his feet, her soft body interlaced with his ankles. He looked down. The sludgy substance had coated her naked body, and now there was blood slathered everywhere, plastered on the smooth white surface of the bathtub. She was screaming, the shrill sound ripping through his eardrums like a dart.

Richard's heart was racing. What the *fuck* was happening? What the fuck was this shit? The rancid stench told him that this was some kind of sewerage. But why was it melting the flesh from his bones like acid?

Olivia was grabbing at his legs. His feet slipped in the bloody shit that lined the bottom of the bath. He stumbled forward, the pain becoming too much to bear. His feet slipped from under him. As he fell from the bath, he grabbed onto the glass screen, his weight tearing it from the wall. As it hit the tiled floor of the bathroom, the glass shattered, the broken shards slicing through his raw, bloody skin.

Richard scrambled up to his feet. Olivia was still screaming. She was still in the bath, her body having been semi-buried in the brown, shitty substance, which now filled the bath almost halfway.

But Richard couldn't believe his eyes. It looked as if the shit was moving, slithering over her body, pulsating as it climbed over her.

How was this even possible?

The shit slithered over Olivia's face, slipping into her gaping mouth, choking her. Blood poured from her nostrils.

Richard needed to help her. He *had* to. Despite his own skin having been shredded by the shit, he couldn't just leave her to be slaughtered by whatever the fuck this stuff was. He grabbed onto her hand and pulled, the blood making it difficult to keep his grip.

A tendril burst from the surface of the shit, long and skinny, like a squid's tentacle. It wrapped around Richard's neck and squeezed, choking him, cutting off the supply of oxygen to his brain. And then something else, something sharp, biting into his neck. Razor sharp teeth, pointed like the thorns of a rosebush, protruded from the tendril, and sliced through his skin. Blood jettisoned his body via the lacerated arteries.

Richard could feel his body growing weak. He lost his grip on Olivia's blood-slicked hand. He could only watch as her body disappeared under the surface of the shit, now overflowing from the bathtub, innumerable tendrils having now emerged from the mass, crawling up the walls.

It was alive. It was a creature of some kind.

And it was killing them.

***

Lauren dipped her elbow into the water. It was the perfect temperature.

Eddy loved bath time more than anything. He always had. Everybody used to say that he was a real water baby. He had been born a Sagittarius, but he really should've been a Pisces. He was nine months old now, and still he loved playing and splashing in the water.

"Come on then, spud," said Lauren, her precious baby boy sitting on the floor at her feet. "Let's get you washed up."

Eddy gurgled happily as Lauren picked him up and dropped him into the lukewarm water. She selected a bunch of toys from the basket at the side of the bath – a pair of water-squirting rubber ducks, a wind-up mermaid, a plastic boat, a rubber shark – and dropped them into the water with him. Immediately, Eddy snatched them up and began to bounce them through the water.

Lauren had only run the bath to around an inch high – it was all that was needed to bathe Eddy. Still, he was managing to splash it all over the bathroom. "There'll be more water on the floor than there will be in the bath if you carry on like that," laughed Lauren. Eddy smiled up at her, a toothy, happy grin.

Lauren couldn't help but feel entirely elated. She'd always thought she knew what love was, but she hadn't. Not really. Not until Eddy had come along.

She hadn't ever really wanted to have a child. The truth was, she'd never believed that she might make a good mother. Her own parents had been good to her, but she'd just always felt as though this was something that she herself would never be able to replicate.

But then she'd met Dan, and everything had changed.

She loved Dan with all her heart. He was a good man. He looked after her, he gave her everything she could ever want. This was what love was supposed to feel like. Love couldn't possibly get any better than this.

Or so Lauren had thought. But then Eddy came along, and everything got a million times better.

Dan worked nights as a security guard at a shopping centre. That meant that most evenings, Lauren was left all alone with Eddy. But that suited her down to the ground. She loved Eddy more than the world. He was her entire life now.

And bath day was her favourite day. Just to see the joy on her baby's face was enough to melt her heart.

Lauren squeezed a dollop of bath cream onto a sponge. She cupped her hand across Eddy's forehead so as to shield his eyes, then squeezed the sponge over his head. The boy squealed with delight as the water cascaded down his head and over his chubby, little body. Lauren then ran the sponge over his back and his belly, lifting his arms one at a time to get into his armpits.

Her phone was ringing downstairs. "Shit," Lauren muttered under her breath, safe in the knowledge that Eddy wouldn't yet be able to understand her. She had a few years yet, before she would need to curb that sort of language. She'd be mortified were she to ever send him to nursery, only for him to use such language in front of the other kids.

The phone was still ringing.

"Alright, alright," said Lauren, groaning as she pushed herself up on the side of the bath, her knees feeling as if they might belong to an eighty-year-old granny, rather than the *supposedly* spritely young twenty-four year old she was supposed to be. "I'm coming."

Eddy was busy playing with the ducks, dunking them under the water, then allowing them to bob back up to the surface. It wasn't as if the ducks could even be fully submerged in the meagre amount of water that lined the bottom of the tub, but still he was enjoying himself.

He'd be safe in there. It wasn't as if he could drown in the few centimetres of water he'd been allowed.

Of course, Lauren knew this wasn't true – of course he *could* drown – but the chances were entirely slim. Besides, she'd only be gone for a few seconds.

"You wait right here," said Lauren, splashing Eddy with the water. "I'll be right back."

Eddy smiled and babbled nonsensically.

Lauren made her way down the stairs and, as sod's law would always have it, the phone stopped ringing the moment her fingertips glanced across it. It was as if somebody were watching her through the window, and hung up at the precise moment that would cause the most annoyance.

Still, Lauren picked up the phone and checked the missed call. It was her sister, Louisa. She decided to call her back.

Louisa answered on the first ring. "Hey, bitch," she said, the rudeness somewhat expected, what with the two siblings having teased each other the entirety of their lives. "How's it going?"

"Not bad," said Lauren. "What about you?"

"Oh, you know. Same shit, different day. But enough about me… How's our little superstar doing?"

Lauren didn't need to ask Louisa to whom she was referring. "Eddy's just fine. He's in the bath right now."

"Oh," said Louisa. "I'm sorry. I didn't realise. If you're busy, I can call you back later."

"No," chuckled Lauren. "It's fine. *He's* fine. He loves it in there."

But it wasn't fine.

If Lauren had stayed in the bathroom, she'd have seen the shitty gunk oozing out of the bathtub's overflow pipe. Perhaps then she might've been able to pluck Eddy out of the water before anything bad happened.

Too late for that now.

Lauren continued to talk to her sister as she made her way back up the stairs and into the bathroom.

The sight before her twisted her gut so hard she thought she might vomit blood. But it wasn't blood that came; it was a high-pitched shriek.

The phone tumbled to the floor, Louisa's muffled voice crackling from the earpiece. "Hello? Lauren? What's happening? HELLO?"

The bathtub was almost full, a thick, brown substance having filled it, bright red crimson marbling the surface.

Blood.

Eddy's blood.

The boy's head floated on top of the shit, splattered with blood, his glassy eyes staring at the ceiling. The skin had been partly peeled from the side of his face, revealing his tiny, delicate skull beneath. One of his eyeballs had seemingly been torn from the socket. Worse still, it was clear to Lauren that his head was no longer attached to his body; a hand protruded from the surface of the slimy shit-water, at the other end of the tub, at least four feet away. The toes of one of his dismembered feet poked out of the shit somewhere in the middle.

Feces Of Death

Lauren was still screaming.

She dropped to her knees and plunged her hands into the filth, ignoring the vile stench that wafted into her nostrils, digging through the feces in hopes of pulling her baby out. She just wanted to cuddle him, to cradle him in her arms.

But her arms couldn't move. The substance was thick, like how she imagined hardening concrete might feel were one submerged up to the elbows. But it wasn't this that prevented her arms from moving – it was something else. Something *within* the shit, holding onto her. It was alive; she could feel it moving, the soft, malleable waste material pulsating around her skin. It was as if it was breathing.

Still screaming, her breathing racked, Lauren sobbed as she watched a tendril of shit emerge from the faecal mound and slither into Eddy's mouth, dragging his decapitated head under the surface.

And then there were more tendrils, dancing from the surface of the shit like tamed cobras. Some of them were split down the middle, peeling open like bananas, revealing rows of what Lauren could only imagine were teeth, thin and pointed, like those of a cat. One of the tendrils had a long, hooked claw protruding from the end. It was thick and curved, like an eagle's talon. It was this claw that slashed forward, slicing open Lauren's throat.

Lauren fell face first into the bathtub, face first into the shit, her own blood mixing with that of her dead baby's.

***

Kelly's mother had always told her that boys were only after one thing. Kelly herself had never been entirely sure what she was supposed to *do* with this information. Was she supposed to avoid boys altogether? Never talk to them? Never even look at them?

Her mother had been right, of course; boys *did* only want one thing from her. But, as far as Kelly was concerned, that was fine. She enjoyed the attention she received from boys, the way they looked at her, how they desired her, how they wanted to do bad things to her. It was exciting. Ever since puberty had hit, members of the opposite sex had swarmed around her constantly.

She had been blessed with her mother's genes, meaning that, once her hormones had kicked in, her body had become shapely almost overnight. Her breasts had filled out to a firm B cup, and her buttocks had taken a rounder, more voluptuous form. Pair that with her skinny, slender waist, and this was a body to kill for.

Kelly was only sixteen. She was the most popular girl in school. So many boys wanted to date her… or… wanted to fuck her. But, so far, Kelly had managed to keep her virginity fully intact. Not that she was a prude of any kind, and she sure got horny herself. But she wasn't just going to give it up to any spotty, lustful teenager. She wanted to feel loved.

But, perhaps she wouldn't have much choice in the matter.

Yes, Kelly's mother had always warned her about boys. But, like many a rebellious teenager, Kelly thought she knew best. Naturally, when her mother told her *not* to go to any parties where there would be

Feces Of Death

drugs and alcohol and teenage boys looking to take advantage of her, Kelly had chosen to *not* heed those warnings.

So far, this hadn't caused her too many problems. But tonight was different. Tonight, she had drunk far too much. She was wasted, to the point that she could barely stand. It was for this reason that, when she had informed him that she was about to puke, Callum had offered to escort her to the bathroom.

The party was at Cindy's house. Her parents were away, so Cindy had taken the opportunity to throw a killer party. She'd invited nearly the entire school year, even the nerdy kids, as – in her exact words – it was always good to broaden one's social horizons. In fact, as far as Kelly had known, only two people had failed to get an invite – Cindy's ex-boyfriend Ricky, and Chloe, the dumb bitch he'd cheated on her with.

Callum was there too, of course. He was, as Cindy would describe him, Kelly's 'love interest'. Kelly herself didn't see him that way. Sure, he was hot, and he wanted to get into her pants just like every other boy she knew, but that didn't make him boyfriend material. Far from it.

But he'd always seemed nice enough. Perhaps that was why he was helping her now, assisting in her ascent of the stairs, towards the bathroom. Surely, he had no more nefarious reasons in mind.

Kelly leant against the sink, breathing deeply, trying desperately to stifle the sensation of vomit creeping up her throat. Yeah, Callum might not be boyfriend material, but she still didn't want him seeing her throwing her guts up.

Callum put his hands on Kelly's hips, pushing in close to her. "How are you feeling now?" he asked.

Kelly could only shake her head. If she opened her mouth to speak, she knew there was every chance she'd evacuate the contents of her stomach.

"You look really pretty tonight, you know?" whispered Callum.

What was this? Why was he complimenting her now? There was no way she looked good, not with that sickening sensation twisting in her gut. She was probably pale, all the colour drained from her face. She'd have looked at herself in the mirror, if it weren't for the fact that her eyes were clouded by the excess of alcohol she'd consumed.

Callum's hands moved downward, finding a comfortable spot on the side of her bare thighs. Kelly had worn a dress – bright red, the pleated material hugging her curves. She didn't like the feel of Callum's hands on her skin, but she was too inebriated to do anything meaningful about it. No – all of her efforts needed to remain focused on her *not* throwing up.

But then Callum's hand began to gradually slide upwards, under the skirt of her dress.

Kelly turned, knocking his hands away. "N… no," she stuttered, barely able to keep her eyes open. "Don't t… touch me."

Callum ignored her. He took her by the hips again and pushed himself against her. "Why not?" he said, a sly smile on his face. "Come on. I know you want this. The sexual tension has been building between us for, like, forever."

A lump caught in Kelly's throat, the vomit trying to force its way past her sphincter. "No," Kelly repeated, dangerously close to spewing. "N… no…

Feces Of Death

no. I don't. I def… definitely don't. No. Not. At. All…"

Callum reached under her dress once again, his hands sneaking higher this time, so that his fingertips slid across the banding of her underwear. "Kiss me."

"No. I… I don't w… want to."

"Yes you do."

Callum pushed his hips into Kelly's. She could feel the bulge in his jeans, his stiffening erection pressing against the inside of the denim. She wasn't completely sexually inactive; she'd given enough hand jobs and blowies to know what a boner felt like.

Kelly snorted. "Me and you… W… We are not… having… sex."

"How much do you want to bet?" said Callum, chuckling to himself. His hand was between her legs then, rubbing her vagina through the thin material of her panties.

Kelly went to push him away, but it was all too much. An agonising contraction squeezed at her insides, causing her to double over. She dropped to her knees, scrambled to the toilet, and promptly vomited, her stomach feeling as if it were folding inside out, the burning, acidic bile tearing along her oesophagus.

Despite her current state, Callum wasn't about to take no for an answer. It was about time this little cock tease got what she was asking for.

He dropped to his knees behind her prone form, her back arching with every torrid expulsion of vomit. He lifted her dress and flipped it up onto the back, exposing her pert arse, beautifully clad in her white cotton panties. He hooked his fingers over the waistband of said panties, and pulled them down until they rested on the backs of her knees.

There it was, that tight, juicy slit. Callum had no idea if anybody had ever buried their dick in there before, and, to be quite honest, he didn't much care either way. Kelly was completely shaved, and that meant that she was absolutely expecting to get some cock tonight.

He unbuttoned his jeans and pulled out his erection. He spat into the palm of his hand, then slathered it along the shaft. He then lined himself up and forced himself into Kelly.

Kelly groaned as Callum's thick cock penetrated her. Again she retched, more vomit spattering the inside of the toilet bowl.

She was so tight. The walls of her pussy gripped Callum's member like a vice. He pumped in and out, reaching around to grab a handful of her juicy tits. Not once did Kelly object, so that meant she was enjoying it (well, as much as she possibly *could* enjoy, now that she was practically unconscious, face down in the toilet).

Kelly wasn't moving anymore. Callum felt sure that she had fallen unconscious. No matter; he'd be finished soon enough anyway. Three more thrusts, then he came, squirting his slimy semen into her sodden twat.

He pulled out. "Oh, yeah," he sighed as he slapped her buttocks, a short, sharp slap he felt sure would elicit some sort of response. Kelly didn't move an inch. "Sorry babe, but I didn't get a chance to put a rubber on. You might need to get an abortion in a couple of months!" He was laughing then, hoping that she might see the funny side too.

Feces Of Death

But Kelly didn't say a word. She didn't move a muscle. She didn't even take a breath.

"Kelly?"

Callum pushed Kelly to one side. She slumped onto the bathroom floor, rolling onto her back.

Horrified by what he saw, Callum clamped a hand to his mouth.

Kelly's face was gone. And not figuratively speaking – not like she was so paralytic that her soul no longer inhabited her body. No – her face was *literally* gone. The entire front half of her head was missing, the flesh and the skull having been torn away. Even her brain was gone. All that remained of her head was the hollow, concave structure at the back of her cranium, the bone slick with blood.

In the toilet, a mound of shit had filled the bowl. In the middle of the shit was a hole, like a puckered sphincter. It pulsed in and out, as if it were trying to swallow. Inside the hole, rows of pointed teeth trailed downward. The shit then folded out of the toilet, turning inside out like a prolapsed anus, expanding towards the ceiling. Those teeth that had lined the inside of its throat now littered the outside of its form, the brown mass swelling, undulating waves distorting the surface in concentric rings.

"What the fu…"

Callum's words were cut short as the shit monster sprang forward, engulfing him. Callum tried to scream as the teeth ripped into his flesh and scraped against the bones beneath, but there was no air inside the creature. He couldn't even breathe.

Not that it really mattered now.

He was dead a few seconds later anyway.

***

The shits emerged from the sewers in great swarms. They varied vastly in shape and size. Some were as big as a large man, while others were the size of a dog. Some had wide, gaping maws full of razor-sharp shark's teeth. Others seemed to be entirely formless, malleable blobs of excrement. Most had long tendrils protruding from their bodies, with which they dragged themselves along. Those which didn't seemed to squirm along the ground, dragging their bodies behind them like slugs or worms.

One thing they all seemed to have in common was a hunger for human flesh.

As they oozed from the sewers via toilets and sinks and drains, they attacked whomever they fell upon, stripping the flesh from their bones, drinking their blood, consuming their corpses. Savage teeth tore through skin and scraped against bone, severing limbs from weaker bodies. Nobody was safe from the wrath of the shits.

One of the monsters slithered out of a storm drain, its shapeless mass blocking the road. A car swerved to miss it, the driver unsure of *what* he was seeing, no doubt. But, with his eyes fixed on the mound of feces that seemed to be rolling along the road, he crashed his car into a second, stationery vehicle. Dazed, the driver climbed from his car, only to be immediately attacked by the creature he'd tried so hard to avoid. It dragged him to the ground, two claws digging into his stomach like daggers. They tore open his flesh, his viscera leaking out through the cavernous wound.

Several of the monsters pushed their way out of a drain in the middle of a children's playground. Being as late as it was, most of the town's kids were tucked up in bed, safe and sound. But a small group of teenagers had gathered here to smoke some weed. There were two boys and two girls, the boys no doubt hopeful that they might get some action later into the evening. But that wasn't to be, as the monsters tore them to shreds with ease. They bit one of the boys' head clean off his shoulders, jagged teeth tearing through his neck as if it were nothing more than string cheese. The others tried to run, but it was of little use. Tendrils sprang from the shits and wrapped around them, dragging them back to meet their doom.

Even animals weren't safe. A trio of the shits made their way onto a farm on the outskirts of town. There, they entered the sheep's paddock, and began to feast of the tender lamb. When the farmer was altered by the shrill wails of his beloved animals, he ran out there, shotgun in hand, ready to kill whatever it was that was attacking them – to his mind, it was a fox most likely. But the shits ate him too, the three shots he managed to get off before his death having no effect on the creatures, their soft bodies absorbing the pellets as if they were nothing.

Countless people died in those first moments after the shits emerged from the sewers. The monsters showed no mercy. They forced their way into people's homes and consumed those they found within. Men, women and children – all were slaughtered by the shits, their carcasses mulched by the creatures' terrible jaws.

Piles of the dead remained wherever the shits had been, trails of blood and faecal matter smeared along the floor the only indication of where they were headed next…

CHAPTER TWELVE
Home Invasion

Emily had tried to call Martin several times over the past hour or so. It wasn't like him to be so late. It had just gone seven; he was due back over two hours ago. Emily found herself growing worried as time continued to tick by and she heard nothing back. She was sure everything was fine; he was just undoubtedly busy. But if that were the case, then surely he'd have let her know. That was what he'd normally do.

Perhaps he was just too busy to even answer her calls, or to send her a text, just to let her know he was okay.

God, that was stupid. What in the hell was she worried about? He'd told her he was snowed under; of course he was still working. That was it. He really was just too busy.

Well – just so long as they were paying him his overtime.

She decided to make herself a drink. She lifted the kettle from the kitchen side and carried it over to the sink. There, she turned the tap and waited, the pipes banging momentarily as the water babbled from the spout. This lasted only a few seconds before the water started to flow properly again.

Great, she thought to herself. *Another problem for Martin to look at once he got home.*

Where in the hell was he anyway?

She set the kettle to boil, then pulled her phone from her pocket, intending to try and call him once again. She swiped up on the screen, and…

Shit. It was dead. When had that happened? Jesus… Maybe Martin *had* tried to call her back after all…

Emily retrieved the length of phone charger cable from behind the toaster and plugged it into the bottom of her phone, waiting to ensure that a proper connection was made. Satisfied that all was as it should be, she set her phone on the windowsill and proceeded to make herself a cup of coffee.

She sat and watched about five minutes of a soap opera, before deciding that she ought to try Martin again. She went back into the kitchen and retrieved her phone from the windowsill. She switched it on and, once it had booted up, opened up her contacts list and called Martin once more.

Again, he didn't answer.

This time, she decided to leave a message: "Martin? Where are you? You should've finished work…" - she checked the clock hanging on the kitchen wall - "…nearly three hours ago now. Please call me back. I'm starting to get worried. Okay. Bye." She hung up, hoping that Martin would either return her call soon, or that he'd simply come strolling in through the front door. Perhaps he might be a little drunk, having gone for a few beers after work. It wasn't something he'd ever done before, but there was a first time for everything, right?

Something in Emily's gut told her that something was wrong.

No. She was just being silly. She needed to relax. She should take a bath. That would calm her nerves.

If Martin turned up soon enough, perhaps he could even join her.

Emily headed upstairs, and into the bathroom. Leaning over the side of the bath, she clicked the plug into the plughole, then turned on the tap.

The pipes banged once again, rattling in whatever the fixings were that kept them attached to the floorboards. The copper rattled at the water chugged along. Then a sputter of dirty water coughed into the bottom of the tub.

Quickly, Emily shut off the tap. Why was the water so dirty? She couldn't bathe in that; it was disgusting. She pulled the plug and watched as the brown substance slithered away down the drain.

A clunking noise came from behind her. Emily turned. It had come from the toilet. It sounded like there was something alive inside the cistern. She stepped a little closer and listened as the clunk came again, the sound obscured by the thick porcelain.

She lifted the top from the cistern and looked inside, half expecting to find a rat – or something similarly grotesque – to be trapped inside (not that she had any idea how a rat might've gotten in there in the first place). She found no such thing. Instead, she saw a series of bubbles emerging from the base of the filler valve – at least, she believed that this was what she was looking at. Whatever it was, it must've been broken.

Great.

Was that what had been causing the banging noises coming from the pipes? Maybe. Emily couldn't possibly know for sure; this was well beyond her area of expertise. For a moment, she considered reaching in there and having a feel around the offending part, to see if she might possibly be able to find the source of the bubbles. But she quickly decided against this course of action; she wouldn't know what to do, even if she found something. No – Martin would need to take a look once he got home.

Emily returned the lid to the cistern. She looked down into the bowl and noticed a brown-ish mist circling up from out of the u-bend. Feeling a slight sense of disgust, she flushed the toilet, ignoring the fact that Martin had told her not to due to the potential blockage, and closed the seat.

She left the room, switching off the light as she went.

But then, the moment the lights went out, a loud thud emanated from somewhere behind her, inside the bathroom, causing her heart to skip a handful of beats, racing then to catch back up to itself. In the back of her mind, she recognised the sound as one she'd heard countless times before – the toilet seat having been dropped, and allowed to collide with the rim of the bowl. But that couldn't be the source of the sound; she'd lowered the seat just a few short moments ago. One thing she knew for certain – that hadn't been the pipes.

Slowly, apprehensively, Emily turned and looked back into the bathroom. She switched on the light.

Nothing.

Everything was exactly as it had been when she'd turned her back, not five seconds ago.

Of course it was. Why wouldn't it be?

Suddenly, the toilet seat lifted just half an inch, then dropped back down, clattering as it bounced from the porcelain.

Emily's heart leapt into her throat. *What the hell was that?*

It happened again, the toilet seat rattling, the plastic-coated MDF bouncing up and down, as if something *inside* the toilet was trying to push its way out, but was too weak to lift the seat fully.

Clack. Clack clack. ClackClackClack. ClackClackClackClackClack!

Emily's heart was thundering in her chest. Her limbs felt weak, as if they'd turned to jelly. But that was silly; there was nothing to be scared of. It was a rat. It *had* to be a rat. Martin had mentioned such a thing happening to somebody else, just yesterday. Sure, that in and of itself was disgusting; the thought of having some sodden rodents scattering around in her bathroom made her stomach turn. But what was she supposed to do? Flush it away? Rats weren't scary. They might've been fucking vile, repulsive little creatures, but they weren't scary.

Trembling, she stepped forward. A foot or so back from the toilet, she reached out with her bare foot and slid her toes into the narrow gap between the seat and the rim. With her foot now wedged unto the seat, she flicked her leg upward, flipping open the seat.

Horror slammed into Emily's chest. Confusion gnawed at her bones.

There were no rats.

It was something else. For a moment, Emily assumed that the pipes were backing up again, a mountain of human excrement being forced out of the sewers, up through her pipes, and out via her toilet, the noxious odour filling the room. But then she noticed something different about it, something unusual. It was moving. A shimmering, pulsating mound of shit! It was swelling, expanding, seeping out over the rim of the toilet.

Emily could hardly breath. She could hardly believe what she was seeing. Were her eyes somehow playing tricks on her? How was any such thing even possible? It *wasn't* alive; it *couldn't* be. Something was forcing the feces out of the toilet, and causing it to move like that, air trapped in the waste pipes, or something.

But then she saw the tentacles, slick with stringy slivers of crap, growing out of the amorphous mass, slithering across the floor, dragging the mound out of the toilet bowl, like some kind of hideous octopus. But these tentacles weren't lined with suction cups like those of an octopus – they were lined with rows of pointed spines.

And then, before Emily even knew what was happening, one of those tentacles whipped out, and wrapped around her forearm, the needle-sharp spines digging into her flesh.

Emily gasped. She tried to pull her arm free, but the thing – whatever *the fuck* it was – held on tight. Emily's struggles only served to cause the spines to dig in further. Her arm went numb as blood began to trickle down over her wrist.

The blob of shit began to stretch and distort, reshaping itself into a taller, skinnier form. Part of the thing split open in an upside-down 'V' shape, the bottom half peeling away to reveal innumerable teeth. They were short and stubby, like those of a crocodile. Emily couldn't help but think that this was this creature's mouth. It was then that she noticed what looked like a small yellow bead, planted in the malleable substance. Was that its *eye*? Was it *looking* at her?

This was insane. The flesh of her arm was being shredded by a mound of mutant shit!

Emily screamed. She pulled at her arm, not caring about the additional damage being inflicted. She flailed her free arm, groping for something close by, anything that might help her free herself. But there was nothing; she had insisted that the bathroom be clean and tidy and free of clutter at all times. Instead of some kind of weapon, she found her hand landing on the doorframe. She grabbed on tight and pulled, hoping that the extra leverage might allow her to free herself.

But the creature was too strong. It fought back, pulling her in towards its ravenous, gaping maw.

Emily's fingers slipped from the doorframe. She tumbled forward, crashing into the beast, its soft body moulding around her momentarily. The impact caused her to stumble sideways, her free hand once again scrambling for something to hold onto. Her elbow slammed into the medicine cabinet, the glass door shattering, the shards cascading down into the sink below. The whole cupboard came away from the wall, the contents spilling across the floor. Numerous pill bottles split open, the little white tablets inside scattering across the bathroom floor.

Emily noticed that some of the tablets had landed right next to one of the tentacles. As the shit monster slithered towards her, that tentacle ran over those pills. As soon as it did, the creature pulled its tentacle away, hissing. The stink of burning feces filtered up Emily's nostrils, threatening to make her vomit.

But she held it down. There was something more important here. Those pills had seemingly *burned* the monster, and it had seemingly felt pain.

Downstairs, the front door slammed shut. Emily was forever telling Martin not to slam the door; he was just *so* heavy-handed. But, right now, she didn't care. Martin was home – that had to be him. "Emily?" Martin bellowed up the stairs, a prang of relief tugging at Emily's heart. "Honey? Are you here?"

Emily wanted to reply. She *intended* to reply. But when she opened her mouth, no words came out. Instead, she screamed.

She reached down and scooped up a handful of the scattered pills, and pushed them into the side of the creature's head…

It's head… This was fucking crazy. Did this thing even have a head? Emily had aimed for the yellow pinhole she'd assumed was its eye. Whatever it was she hit, the fecal matter beneath her palm began to melt, sizzling as the pills burned through its ordurous flesh.

Martin and David burst into the bathroom just in time to see the creature roar – a wet, guttural sound – and release its grip on Emily's arm.

Feces Of Death

"Holy fuck!" said David "Those arseholes weren't kidding!"

The monster slithered away, back down the toilet, dirty water forming a putrid lake over the bathroom floor.

Emily dropped to the floor, clutching her injured arm, her back propped against the bath.

Martin rushed over to her, dropping to his knees beside her. "Oh my God!" he said, panic flooding his voice. "Are you okay?"

Emily reluctantly gave up her arm for him to inspect. "It bit me," she whimpered, tears now streaming down her cheeks. "That fucking thing bit me!"

Martin turned her arm over, checking her wounds. Emily herself could barely look. When she did, she was greeted by the grizzly sight of a dozen puncture wounds lining her arm. Blood leaked from the lacerations, spattering the tile.

"What did you do to it?" asked David.

"What do you mean?" said Emily.

"It looked as if you hurt it. You scared it away. How did you do that?"

Emily shook her head. "The pills. It must've been the pills. It was as if they… they burnt it, somehow."

David bent and picked up one of the broken pill bottles. He turned it over and read the label. "No fucking way… Laxatives. They're fucking laxatives!"

Emily looked into David's eyes, grateful that he was there with her now. "You don't seem all too surprised to find that a giant pile of shit was trying to kill me."

Martin smiled. "No. We may have been pre-warned."

"By whom?"

"By the people who made these things."

"These... *things*?" said Emily, her eyebrows raised. "You mean there's more than just this one?"

Martin shrugged his shoulders. "We don't know. The guy we spoke to - he didn't seem too sure himself."

"So," said David. "What do we do now?"

Martin took a moment to think. He was pressing onto Emily's wounds, preventing her from losing any more blood than she already had. It hurt, but she didn't mind; she was just glad that he was there.

"It looks like laxatives are the best weapon we have against them," said Martin. "We should go get some more."

"And then what?"

"Then, I guess we go and find those PharmaCom guys, and tell them everything we know."

CHAPTER THIRTEEN
Subterranean Assault

William Harper – better known to his friends and colleagues as Bill – had been in his current job for over thirty years, and in all that time, never had he experienced anything quite so bat-shit crazy as this. Granted, he'd seen some insane crap come out of those PharmaCom labs before, but this… This was something else.

Bill was ex-military. He'd seen all manner of conflict. He'd toured in Afghanistan and Iraq. He couldn't even remember the number of times his life had been on the line, an unseen enemy all but ready to snuff him out.

But *those* enemies had always been human. What he'd been sent here to deal with was something entirely different.

They'd briefed him before he and his team had left for this small southern town, so that they might know what it was they were going up against. This wasn't the sort of situation they were used to having to deal with. They were the security team; they were *supposed* to protect the PharmaCom facility. That was it. They were trained to fight, sure, but not against inhuman monsters. There was always a risk that armed gangs would try to break into places such as PharmaCom; the abundant chemicals stored there, including many precious metals, were extremely valuable. Bill had once heard of a company in China losing more than ten millions dollars' worth of stock to armed robbers. PharmaCom couldn't allow that to happen to them.

As such, they had a specialist team of security officers, and it was *this* sort of threat they had been trained to deal with.

PharmaCom was – as should be plainly obvious by the company's entirely on-the-nose name – a pharmaceutical company. For the most part – and as far as the public were concerned – their primary business was the production of cosmetics, although they were also a relatively big player in the field of medicine. What the public *didn't* know – what *most* people didn't know, even their own employees – was that PharmaCom actually made the majority of their money developing bio-weapons.

Bill assumed that what was happening here in this town was actually down to the bio-weapons division. The story he'd told that plumber earlier – about how this was all down to an anti-aging cream, which worked by resurrecting dead cells – was the exact story the PharmaCom people had told *him*. But Bill didn't believe it, not for one second. That was just a cover story, he was sure of it. Quite how such a story might negate any of their culpability, Bill wasn't sure. But perhaps they didn't care about that all too much. Perhaps they just wanted eyes diverted away from the bio-weapons division.

Feces Of Death

As the commander of the security team, Bill had been granted access to some of PharmaCom's most secret projects. The information divulged to him had been done so on a 'need-to-know' basis. As head of security, apparently, he needed to know.

Part of him wished that he didn't.

In the bio-weapons division, he'd seen men afflicted with all sorts of substances, both manmade *and* naturally derived. He'd seen men have their skin melted from their bones, dissolved by some sort of acidic compound. He'd seen flesh devoured by microscopic insects. He'd seen subjects killed slowly, their final hours spent in torturous agony, as viruses burned through their bloodstream.

Whatever it was – bio-weapon, anti-aging cream, or something entirely different – Bill and his team were there now, and their only goal was to stop these monstrosities from spreading beyond this town, into the neighbouring towns and cities, and infecting the entire goddamned country.

As always, Bill took point. He was now armed with an M4 Carbine assault rifle. A flashlight was attached to the barrel of the gun, cutting through the darkness of the sewer as he dropped through the manhole. His feet almost slipped out from under him as the soles of his boots landed in some slimy, disgusting substance, seemingly coating the entirety of the concrete slab on which he was now standing. "Careful as you climb down," he called up to the others. "I don't want any of you going for a swim right now." He looked at the stream of water flowing just a few inches to his left. Filth and grime floated on its surface, the thought of even dipping his toes in almost causing him to retch.

Anthony Barker climbed halfway down the ladder, before releasing his grip and dropping the remaining three feet. "Don't worry about that," he said to Bill. "No amount of money could get me in that shit."

Bill raised his eyebrows. "If you slip and fall in, no amount of money would get me to get in there and rescue you."

Anthony snorted a laugh.

Sebastian and Jim made their way down the ladder next. Looking at them now, Bill realised that none of them were really equipped for this. They were all still dressed in their white shirts and black ties, each of them having rolled their sleeves up to their elbows. Like Bill, each of them carried an M4 Carbine, a flashlight mounted beneath the barrel. Each of them scanned the tunnels that surrounded them, the torchlight cutting through the darkness as if it were something solid and entirely tangible.

They had entered the sewers via the access point in the car park of the manufacturing company where that guy had died in the toilet, the flesh of his arm having been shredded as if by a school of piranhas. One of his colleagues had found him dead on the bathroom floor, his arm stripped down to bare bone, slathered in blood. Bill had seen photos; it was a gruesome sight. He didn't envy the man who'd stumbled upon it, on his way to take a leak.

But little did he know, he and his men were about to find something much, much worse.

They made their way along the tunnel, lights bouncing from the mould covered walls. As the light danced from the green slime, Bill almost thought that the tunnel looked alive. *Was* it alive? That wasn't possible, was it? No – the stuff that PharmaCom had spilled only had an effect on living cells. It wasn't possible that it had breathed life into the solid concrete of the tunnel, was it?

Fuck, thought Bill. *Anything's possible.*

The four men shuffled their way through the tunnels, sticking to solid walkways that lined either side. Not one of them had any intention of setting foot in the rancid water. They should be directly under the building now, the place that man got killed directly overhead.

But Bill had no idea what they were looking for. He expected that they might find the creature – or *creatures*, he was painfully aware – crawling through the sewers, looking for the next available point of egress, where it might just find its next victim. *Its next meal.* But, so far, there were no signs.

Nothing.

Not until Bill saw the vile excrement smeared along the length of the wall, and spiralling up to the roof.

"What the fuck is that?" muttered Anthony.

"Is that shit?" said Seb.

"This is a sewer," said Jim, the answer obvious. "Of course it's shit - the whole fuckin' place is full of it."

"Yeah, I know. But why the fuck is it on the walls?"

Bill traced the path of the feces along the wall, where it disappeared into the darkness ahead. "Come on," he said. "Let's keep moving."

"Are we following the shit?" asked Seb.

Bill looked at him and nodded.

"Why?"

Bill could feel himself frowning. Why was this guy asking such stupid questions? He knew why they were there. He knew the assignment. He'd signed up for this. Well... Not this exactly. Even Bill himself hadn't signed up for *this*. But this was the job at hand. They needed to find this thing before it killed again. "Whatever it was that killed that poor man up there," he said, pointing the muzzle of his gun up at the roof, to the building beyond. "It's that *thing* that's left this trail. It's our job to find it, and kill it. The only way we're gonna do that, is if we follow its trail. You got that?"

Sebastian nodded. "Man, this is fucked up."

"You think I *want* to be here? Trust me - I don't."

Bill led the men deeper into the sewer system, doing his best to follow the trail that the monster had left behind. He tried to think about what they might do when they found it. They had armed themselves with guns, but Bill wasn't even sure that bullets would work against this thing. Did it even have a brain? Did it have blood in its body? If the answer to either of those questions was yes, then Bill felt sure that this thing could be killed. But, truth be told, he wasn't confident that either of those things might be true.

The men moved silently through the tunnels, not one of them daring to say a word, for fear that any noise may draw the unwanted attention of the creature they were currently hunting. Water dripped from above, splashing into the water, over and over – *plink, plink, plink*. The sound echoed from the walls, combining with sound of shuffled footsteps, filling the sewers with an uncomfortable ambience.

Feces Of Death

A noise came from behind; a strange gargling sound, like a cat, purring as it tore the guts from a mouse.

"What the fuck was that?" grunted Anthony.

Bill squeezed past the other men, to the back of the pack. He shone his light down through the tunnel, looking for whatever it was that was behind them now. Had they missed it? Had they somehow walked straight past it?

No. Bill knew that wasn't the case. There was a much more obvious, and entirely concerning answer; there was more than one of those monsters down there with them.

"Fuck me," whispered Jim. "We need to get out of here."

And then a more terrifying sound – a whisper, which almost didn't sound human.

It *had* come from a man though; Seb was staring down into the water, his face pale, a look of abject fear twisting his features into a grotesque grimace.

A body floated along the surface of the water, face down. It was a man. His clothes were little more than dirty rags, hanging from his frame. Behind him, all around the carcass, blood spread through the green water.

Bill pushed through the others. "Move," he urged them. "Get out of the way!" He dropped to his knees and reached out, using his gun to gain extra distance. He pulled the man in towards himself. Pressing down on one shoulder with the barrel of his gun, the man bobbed up and down, then rolled to his back.

Bill gasped.

"Holy fuck!" said Seb, much too loud.

The man's face had been eaten away. All the skin had been peeled back. The skull was slicked with gore, the man's beady eyes staring out of two blackened sockets. His swollen tongue – more than twice the size of a normal tongue – lopped from the side of the mouth, a large chunk having been torn from the meat, allowing the appendage to fold awkwardly, back onto itself.

Bill stood. He aimed his gun down the tunnel, the direction from which the carcass had floated.

There were more of them. More corpses. Men and women, even children. Most were piled in the water, while some lay slumped over, onto the concrete walkway. Some had been stripped down to the bone, while others had merely had slivers of flesh peeled from the bodies. All were coated in a thick layer of ichor, which seemed to glow iridescent as the beams of the flashlights danced across it.

Bill approached the pile of corpses slowly, trying to process just what he was seeing. There must've been at least fifty bodies there, all stacked on top of one another, their gory, ruined extremities having melded together to form one large mountain of death.

"Please tell me this *thing* didn't do this," mumbled Jim.

Bill thought about it. He was more certain now that there was more than one of the creatures; surely, one of them would never have been able to do this alone. "I don't think there's just *one* of these *things*," he said, looking back over his shoulder. "I think we might be sealing with dozens of them. Maybe more."

Feces Of Death

"What?" said Anthony, the fury still audible through his hushed voice. "You mean to say we're lookin' for more than one of these things?"

"I'm afraid so."

"Well, why the fuck weren't we told that before we came down here?"

Seb had continued on. His light flashed across the mound of mangled humanity. There was a young boy amongst the bodies, his skin pale, the top of his head having been torn open, his brain leaking out of his cracked skull. There was a priest, his cossack torn, his body bisected at the waist, his innards leaking from the gaping wound where his pelvis used to be. There was a woman. She was naked. Why was she naked? She must've been nude when that beast had dragged her down here. Seb couldn't help but look at her body, his eyes drawn to her pallid breasts. She'd have been quite the looker, had she still been alive. Her face wasn't bad either, with her soft skin, and her plump lips, and her…

The woman's eyes flicked open as she gasped for air, blood oozing from her mouth, seeping over those beautiful plump lips.

Seb screamed. His arms pinwheeled as he lost his balance. Bill darted towards him, hoping to grab him, to prevent his fall, but it was too late. Seb hit the water with an almighty splash.

"Somebody help her!" yelled Bill, nodding his head towards the blood-soaked woman, trapped in the pile of bodies. Both Jim and Anthony scurried past him and started to dig through the mangled meat, in order to pull the naked woman out. By the time they got to her, she was already dead, having used her last breath to scare the living piss out of Seb.

Seb was thrashing in the water, his head disappearing under the surface, before re-emerging to suck in a deep breath. Bill stretched his hand out towards him. "Grab on," he said. "I'll pull you back up."

Seb struggled to remain afloat, filth and blood and grime and clumps of feces bobbing in the water around him.

Bill stretched further. His fingers brushed against Seb's, but neither of them managed to grab on to the other successfully. Bill tried once again. His hand slipped into Seb's palm.

A shit monster burst from the water then, its wide mouth filled with a million teeth, engulfing Seb, tearing through his flesh, dragging him back down under the water. Seb's screams lasted no longer than a second, then he was gone.

"Holy fuck!" screamed Anthony.

None of the men saw the soft, viscous fluids squeezing out from the writhing pile of human corpse, pushing its way between the bodies, re-forming itself into one of those vile monstrosities.

Before anybody knew what had happened, that creature had taken a hold of Jim and had torn his head from his shoulders.

Anthony whipped around, screaming at the top of his lungs. He took aim and fired, round after round bursting from his Carbine, the bullets landing indiscriminately, tearing through his friend's body, shredding his flesh. Those bullets that did so happen to impact the monster had no effect. They tore through the malleable construction of its formless body – in through the front and out through the back – without eliciting so much as the slightest reaction.

"Come on!" shouted Bill. "We need to get out of here! We need to go, right fucking now!" He grabbed Anthony by the shoulder and pulled him back.

They were running then, their feet slipping precariously on the wet, slimy ledge underfoot.

Behind him, Bill heard Anthony scream.

He turned quickly, only to be greeted by the sight of Anthony floating before him.

No. He wasn't floating; he was being *lifted*. A filthy tentacle had wrapped around his neck and was dragging him upward. Blood poured from the gashes inflicted to his throat as he choked to death.

Bill raised his gun.

His light found a home on the squirming mass of shit that had seemingly adhered to roof of the tunnel. There was no telling how many of the creatures were up there; it may have been one, it may have been a hundred. But there were numerous mouths, all full of razor-sharp sharp teeth. And there were thousands of tentacles, thousands of... *What?* Were they *eyes?*

Bill pulled the trigger of his Carbine, screaming as the creatures began to slither from the roof, descending upon him.

CHAPTER FOURTEEN
Supplies

"Are you okay?" asked Martin, as he tied the bandage around Emily's arm, pulling it tight. He wasn't sure if it was enough to stop the bleeding entirely, but it would have to do until they could get her to a hospital.

Martin could tell that Emily's smile was forced. "I'm fine," she said, nodding her head.

But Martin knew she *wasn't* fine; how could she be? She'd just been attacked by some savage beast, constructed from shit, which had crawled out of their toilet. Even as Martin thought about it now, it was completely insane. How was this even possible?

It didn't matter *how*. All that mattered was that these things were there, and that they somehow needed to try and stop them.

Martin stood, and helped Emily up to her feet. They had been sitting on the bathroom floor. Emily hadn't wanted to sit on the toilet, even with the seat down. Martin couldn't really blame her.

David was waiting for them downstairs. "So?" he said, as the two of them made their way into the kitchen. "What happens next?"

Feces Of Death

Martin looked at Emily and found that she was already looking at him. They locked eyes, and remained that way for what Martin felt was an inordinate amount of time. But that was fine; it gave him a chance to study her, to try and figure out what she was thinking, what she *wanted* him to do.

Emily, like most women, was difficult to read. Most people considered Martin himself to be an open book. But not Emily; she was firmly closed, the pages sealed tight.

With no indication toward what she was thinking, Martin turned back to David. "We need to find these things," he said. "We need to kill them."

David shook his head, his eyes rolling. "And how would you suggest we do that?" he said.

Martin looked back to Emily, hoping for just the slightest indication as to what she might be thinking. She was clutching her injured arm against her chest. She looked frightened, but that was understandable, given the circumstances. Martin would never want to force her to do anything she didn't want to do. If she wanted to stay at home and let somebody else deal with this problem – let the professionals clean up their own mess – then he was more than happy to do so.

But then, before he himself had a chance to respond, Emily looked to David and said - "It was the laxatives. We need more laxatives."

Martin smiled. When Emily glanced his way, he offered her a slight nod, wordlessly letting her know that he was proud of her, and that they were doing the right thing.

"Right. Okay. So…" David murmured. "Where do we get them from?"

Martin thought for a moment. There weren't many options. In fact, there was only one place that he could think of, that might be a viable option. "There's a pharmacy in the local shopping centre," he said, his voice lifting, as if this might be the beginning of the end for those repulsive beasts. "We can go there, see what they have."

David checked his watch. "I think they'll be closed now."

With everything that had gone on, Martin had completely lost track of the time. He checked his own watch and saw that it was already eight-fifteen. But that didn't matter; Martin had no intention of walking in there and asking to *buy* all their stock of laxatives. "So, we break in," he said.

David scoffed at the idea, shaking his head furiously. "We can't do that! We're not criminals!"

"I don't think they'll mind. We need this stuff if we're gonna have any chance of fighting these things. We just go in there, and take what we want. They'll thank us for it tomorrow."

"They'll *thank* us? For *stealing* from them? Are you fucking insane? They'll have us locked up!"

"Oh, who gives a shit!" said Emily, a deep frown creasing her forehead. "We have to stop these things. If we don't, who knows how many people might die."

David grumbled. "Fine."

"So, we're doing this?" said Martin, almost unable to believe that Emily had convinced David so easily, and unsure that he even wanted to go through with this himself.

"Looks that way, doesn't it?"
Emily nodded.

"Alright then," said Martin. "Let's get going. The sooner we get what we need, the sooner we can put an end to these bastard things."

David snorted, a half-assed laugh. "You make it sound so simple."

"Fingers crossed, it will be."

***

It took them just fifteen minutes to walk the mile-and-a-half to the shopping centre, having decided that it would actually take them longer to drive there. They didn't see a single other person the entire way there. On more than one occasion, Martin considered that they should perhaps be knocking on people's doors, warning them of the danger that they might be in. But then, he knew that doing so would only cause unnecessary panic.

Was it unnecessary? Perhaps people *ought* to be panicking. Maybe that was how they were going to stay alive.

No. They needed to keep moving. They didn't have time to stop and check in on everybody.

Where was everybody?

Dead already?

Martin really hoped not.

The residential streets through which they'd hurried soon morphed from regular rows of semi-detached houses, into giant blocks of bricks and mortar; tall structures containing dozens of small apartments. These blocks then blended seamlessly into the shopping centre.

There were various shops there in the centre – a barbershop, a fish-and-chip shop, a newsagent, a pizzeria, a post office. Most seemed to be closed. Only the newsagent had any lights on inside. Looking in through the window as they passed, Martin saw no signs of life. It was as if everybody had just disappeared, like the crew of the Mary Celeste abandoning their ship.

Still, that didn't matter, as, right there, in the corner of the centre, was the pharmacy.

A small poster had been stuck to the inside of the glass door, so that it could be read from the outside. Coincidentally, as if it were some kind of a sign, the poster was advertising a new laxative product. A cartoon illustration showed a man sitting on a toilet, his cheeks bright red as he strained to empty his bowels. Above the illustration were the words: 'Don't have a relapse… Re-Lax.' Below the image was a massive block of small print. Martin didn't even try to read it, although one sentence did jump out at him: A PharmaCom Product.

"You're never gonna believe this," said Martin, pointing at the text at the bottom of the poster.

Emily read it, and rolled her eyes.

David read it. "You've gotta be fuckin' kidding me…" He then hurled the brick he was carrying through the pharmacy window, before reaching in through the newly formed opening, and unlocking the door. It amused Martin to think that, just a few short minutes ago, David had been completely reluctant to do this. Now here he was, the main offender, the one who had actually committed the crime of breaking and entering.

Inside, the entirety of the shop was bathed in thick black shadows. Martin had anticipated this, so had found a torch for each of them. The one he was using for himself was his trusty headtorch; the LED light source mounted to an elasticated strap and affixed to his forehead. "I'm not exactly sure *where* we should be looking," he said. "So just take a look around, see what you can find."

David scanned across the shelves, illuminating the boxes of medicine with his own torch. "Even if we find something here," he said, all the while continuing to look. "I'm not sure there's going to be enough."

He was right, of course. What good would a few boxes of pills be? Emily had ground a whole handful into the side of that monster's head, and, although it *had* appeared hurt, it was still far from being dead. "You're right," agreed Martin. "We're gonna need a lot. They must have supplies out back."

"I'll go take a look," said Emily, making her way behind the counter, using her own torch to guide her.

Martin and David continued to scan the shelves. "Ah," said David, a few moments later. "Found them."

Martin crossed the shop, to where David was crouched down, reading from the back of a small, rectangular box. "You think that'll work?" Martin asked.

"How should I know?" said David. "Laxatives are laxatives, as far as I'm concerned. I've never really considered the possibility of having to kill mutant shit monsters with them."

Martin smiled, nodding his head, fully understanding the absurdity of the situation in which they had found themselves.

"Hey guys!" Emily called from the storage room at the back of the shop. "I think we've hit the jackpot here!"

Martin and David both stood, hurrying back to the storeroom. There, Emily was standing before an entire rack stacked floor to ceiling with all different brands of laxative. She flashed her light over them. "Take your pick."

Martin looked over the selection. There were tablets. There were liquids. There were dissolvable powders. He had no idea which would be best when it came to combating the creatures that now plagued the sewers beneath their feet. "Alright. So… I guess we just need some way to… erm… *weaponize* this lot."

Emily snorted. "Right. Any suggestions?"

"Hang on," said David. "I've got an idea." He turned and left the storeroom, and made his way out of the pharmacy.

Martin looked to Emily. "How's your arm?" he asked her.

Emily did her best to smile. "It's okay, I think. I'm not in any pain, really."

"That's good."

"Do you really think this is going to work?" Emily asked, a tone of apprehension to her voice.

Martin shook his head. The truth of the matter was, he wasn't all that confident. "Honestly," he said. "I don't know."

When David returned a minute-or-so later, he did so with a bundle of brightly coloured plastic under his arm. It took Martin more than a few moments to wrap his brain around what he was seeing. But then – as soon as he realised just what it was that David was holding – he understood perfectly.

Feces Of Death

"Super Soakers!" smiled David, almost ready to burst into laughter. "We can fill them with the liquid laxatives!"

Martin took one of the bright yellow water guns from David, turning it over in his hands as if it were a real assault rifle. "I mean," he said, pausing briefly to consider his next words. "This is either the best idea I've ever heard, or it's the stupidest. Where did you even get them from?"

"The newsagent," said David, a smug smile on his face. "They sell toys over there too."

"You stole them? And you were worried about breaking into *here*?"

David shrugged his shoulders. "Like you said - I don't think anybody's gonna mind." He handed another of the guns to Emily.

"Well," said Emily. "It *is* fucking stupid. But, bizarrely - I think it might actually work." She pulled a bottle of the liquid laxative off the shelf, unscrewed the cap, and poured the contents into the filler point at the back of the gun. She then pumped the underbarrel pump a few times, and pulled the trigger, obviously pleased with the force with which the creamy substance exited the nozzle.

"Alright," said Martin, hardly able to believe the words he was saying were actually coming out of his mouth. "Looks like we have a plan. Let's gather up as much of this stuff as we can - we need to take as much ammo as possible." He pulled the empty rucksack from his back – he'd brought it with him, knowing full-well that they'd need something to carry their supplies in – flipped it open, then swept his hand across the shelf containing the liquid laxatives, causing them to tumble from the edge, all but a couple of the bottles landing successfully into the bag.

"We good?" asked David, the dumbest question ever uttered in all of human history.

"Yeah," said Martin, swinging the bag back up onto his back. "We're good."

CHAPTER FIFTEEN
(Un)Holy Shits

"So, where do we start?" asked David, looking to Martin for guidance.

Martin wasn't sure how he had become the designated leader of their little posse. David was *his* boss; perhaps *he* ought to be in charge. But Martin knew David wouldn't want that. David wasn't really the leadership type. He'd only gone for the management job – thus, making him Martin's boss – because he wanted the additional pay. He didn't *actually* want to be in charge. He wasn't an 'ideas man', and he didn't like telling people what to do. He could delegate work, and that was about it. David himself would admit just as much. He would probably even admit that Martin was the better man for the job.

But right now, Martin had no idea where they'd ought to go. He knew they needed to kill these things. But in all the hurry to arm themselves against this immanent threat, he hadn't considered just *where* they would need to go in order to eradicate these monsters.

But then it became all too obvious. "The sewers," Martin said.

The look on the face of both Emily and David told him as much as he needed to know; they didn't like this idea any more than he did.

But that was where the shit monsters had come from. They were coming up from the drains, out of the toilets. The one that had attacked Emily had even retreated back *down* the toilet, back down into the sewers. If they wanted to find these creatures, that was where they needed to look.

But then – where more specifically? There were hundreds – if not thousands – of miles of sewer tunnels running under the town. As best Martin knew, these things had been showing up all over town. There wasn't one spot he could think of, that he could possibly pinpoint as the epicentre of this attack. It might've been under his own house, for all he knew. It might've under his very feet, at that precise moment.

"Would *that* be of any help?" said David, nodding his head off towards something over Martin's right shoulder.

Martin turned, following his line of sight.

Yes, it *would* help. Very much so.

A large, laminated map of the entire town had been mounted on a sign, over by the newsagents. Martin had been into this particular shopping centre on numerous occasions – mostly to collect food from one takeaway or another – and not once had he ever even noticed it. He crossed the centre and stood before the map. It was at least one-and-a-half metres tall by two-and-a-half metres wide. Various points of interest were marked on the map – the lake, the bus station, the candle making museum (something the town was actually famous for), that supersized megamarket that had opened up on the outskirts of town a few years back (and had quickly become a local landmark).

Martin scanned his finger across the map, locating his own home on the east side of town. "This is where *we* live," he said to Emily. "We know there's been an attack there."

"That guy who got killed," said David. "You unblocked his toilet the day before he died – that was Pratchett Road." David pointed to a location all the way over on the other side of town.

"And those PharmaCom guys said somebody else was killed on Lakeshore Industrial Estate." The industrial estate was in the south of town, at least a mile from the actual lake itself.

"But, if all these blockages are actually indicators of where these things are, or where they have been, then I've had reports from all over town. We could look anywhere, and there's every chance we'd just be pissin' in the wind."

"No, no, no. Wait." Martin scanned the map over, three or four times. "I might be nothing, but… No – it makes perfect sense. I know we don't have much data to go by, but look – if we go directly between those three places where we know for certain there's been an attack, look what we find."

David followed Martin's finger as it glided across the map.

"Well, I'll be damned…"

In the middle of the three locations – Hawthorne Road, Pratchett Road, and Lakeshore Industrial Estate – was the sewerage processing plant.

"I think that's as a good a place as any to start," said Martin.

Emily nodded her agreement. "That's settled then. Let's go grab the car – we don't have time to walk all that way."

They made their way back to the house quickly, walking briskly, sometimes even breaking into a jog. The three of them knew that the longer they took, the more likely it was that people might die. Time was of the essence.

Martin drove, Emily beside him in the passenger seat, David in the back.

"Wait," said Emily, as they drove along one of the innumerable roads that snaked through the town, the sharpness of her voice almost causing Martin to jump out of his skin. "What's that?"

Martin followed Emily's line of sight, through the window on her side of the car. Sure enough, out there, beyond the trees, there was a bright light glowing. He knew immediately that this was a fire, raging just a few metres away, turning the purple sky a muddy shade of orange.

"Should we go and look?" said David, leaning forward, between the front seats. "Somebody could need our help."

Martin felt somewhat annoyed, despite knowing that he shouldn't. David was right; somebody out there *could* need their help. Even if there was nobody in any immediate danger there, a fire of that size could spread quickly, consuming everything that crossed its path. The shit monsters could wait, at least for a brief time; the fire could not.

Martin took a sharp left turn, towards the source of the light, blazing through the trees. Despite

Feces Of Death

this being a road on which he'd never driven before, he navigated it easily, following the road as it carved a path into the countryside.

At the top of the hill ahead, there was a church. The roof of the church had partially collapsed, the fire raging inside having chewed through the wooden supports that had once held it in place. Outside the church, a group of people – perhaps fifteen or so; men, women and children alike – were huddled together, watching as the church slowly crumbled, devoured by the fire.

Before them, a priest stood, his arms raised to the heavens.

Martin pulled up alongside them. He exited the car, followed by Emily and David. For a moment, he listened to the priest speak. "Can you not smell it?" he announced. "The stench of excrement always precedes the incursion of the devil!"

"Is everything okay?" Martin asked, feeling a sense of freneticism growing inside. "What happened? Is anybody hurt?"

The group of people all turned to look at him. The priest lowered his arms. "What has happened?" he said, a callous tone to his voice. "Our God has forsaken us, that is what has happened. He has cast us out."

Martin looked to both Emily and David. Both looked just as confused as he felt. "What are you talking about?"

"We are plagued by demons!" said the priest. "Born from the bowels of hell! They have clawed their way out of the underworld, to murder our friends and our families. And our heavenly Father has done nothing to stop them. Like the great plague, and the flood before, He wishes to cleanse this earth, to rid it of all the pain and the suffering caused by mankind."

Martin wasn't at all religious. He knew what this man was saying wasn't true, whether he believed it himself or not. If anything, what the priest was telling these people was nothing short of insane. "No. These creatures, they aren't demons. They haven't come from *hell* – they've come from the sewers. God didn't make them – *people* did, by spilling chemicals into the water supply. But, it's okay. We know how to stop them."

The priest frowned. Martin couldn't tell if he was smiling, or if he was sneering. The gravelly tonality of his voice when he next spoke, told Martin that it was really the latter. "I see what's happening here," the priest said. And then to his congregation – "These people are servants of the devil. They want to prevent God's divine crusade. Take hold of them! Cast them into the fire! Send them back to the hell, from whence they came!"

A murmur echoed amongst the group of people, as they slowly began to stalk toward Martin, Emily and David. Only the children stood back, watching gleefully as the adults approached.

"I swear to God," said David, to the woman nearest to him. "You lay a finger on me, and I'll break your fuckin' legs."

"Martin!" shrieked Emily, as two men descended upon her.

Martin rushed around the car, grabbing one of the men by the shoulder and dragging him away as forcefully as possible. "Get away from her!" Another man was there then, grabbing Martin around the waist, hoisting him from the ground.

Feces Of Death

"That's it, my children!" said the priest. "Let them burn! Burn as they would in the fiery pits of hell!"

The woman continued to stalk towards David. Not one to ever break a promise, he lifted his foot and kicked her square in the chest. "Back the fuck up, bitch! I swear to fucking God…" The woman tumbled backward, the wind forcefully knocked from her lungs. But there were two men on David then, one grabbing each arm and stretching them out wide.

"Do not despair," yelled the priest now, his voice almost engulfed by the roar of the fire behind him. "Do not give up. May the Lord give you strength. Take them! Send them back down to Satan!"

Martin swung his elbow, slamming it into the side of the man's head, loosening his hands from around his waist. But then another man was on him. Together, the two men wrestled Martin to the ground.

Two women grabbed a hold of Emily.

"That's it! Bring them to me! I will cast them into the flames myself! May they burn for all eternity!" The priest was laughing maniacally now, his hands stretched wide, praise be to God.

And then one of those vile creatures burst from the storm drain at his feet, shitty tentacles wrapping around his arms and body.

He couldn't have known that drain was there. No – that wasn't right. Whether he knew about it or not, he was unconcerned about the drain, as he didn't believe that this was where these demons had come from. He believed they had come from hell. His nonsensical beliefs had put him directly in the path of danger.

As the priest screamed, writhing in the grasp of the monster, his parishioners released their grip on their respective captives. For a moment, Martin considered the fact that they had the ability to kill this thing, to save the priest. But why should they? He had wanted *them* dead…

Besides, it was already too late. Blood gushed from the priest's mouth as the monster tore his stomach open with its clawed tendrils, his innards leaking from the gaping wound that was once his belly. One of those tendrils then wrapped around his face, shredding his skin, peeling it away from the skull beneath. His cheeks split wide, extending his lips, exposing his teeth below.

His followers were running then, grabbing their children by the hands, and fleeing into the darkness of the surrounding woodland.

Martin scrambled to his feet, pulling Emily back into the car, firing up the engine, driving away the very moment that David was inside.

"Those fucking maniacs!" yelled David, his cheeks flushed. "They were going to kill us! They were *actually* going to kill us!"

Martin didn't respond. He just wanted to get the hell out of there.

***

The sewerage plant was situated in an industrial part of the town. It was a large, square building, each of the side perfectly perpendicular with each other. It reminded Martin of a giant, grey Rubix cube. There were no windows, save for a few at ground level, next to the reception door. Inside, there appeared to be no lights on. The lack of any signs of life gave the plant an ominous aura.

"Nobody's home," said David, as the car pulled up out front.

"Certainly looks that way," agreed Martin.

"So, what now?" asked Emily.

"I'm not sure," Martin said. "I guess we should just go in and take a look." Martin knew it wouldn't be quite so simple. He knew that, as large as the plant was above ground, it would be twice the size below ground, where all the sewer pipes and tunnels would feed into the processors, delivering their filthy water to be cleaned, and pumped back out into the world. He didn't know where they should even begin.

"Well," said David, lifting his Super Soaker. "I'm ready to do this."

Martin looked to Emily. "And you?" he said, softly. "Are you sure you want to do this?"

Emily nodded. "We have to, don't we?"

Martin smiled. "I guess we do."

Something SLAMMED into the side of the car, colliding with the window, smearing feces over the glass. Emily screamed. So did David. So did Martin.

Whatever it was, it was black. With his vision obscured by the shit streaked across the window, Martin couldn't quite make out if this were one of those monsters or not. But then he saw it; his *wasn't* some amorphous creature… It was a man.

And Martin recognised him.

Quickly, Martin jumped out of the car. The man, plastered head to toe in excrement, rolled onto the bonnet of the car, coughing and spluttering, a thin trail of blood leaking over his lips.

"Bill?" said Martin. "Are you okay? What happened"

The PharmaCom agent straightened up. He wiped the blood away from his mouth with the back of his hand, clearing the shit away from the skin around his lips. "I… It's worse than… than we thought," he stuttered. Panic flickered in his eyes. "Our… our bullets don't stop them. We… we can't kill them!"

"We can," said Martin, grabbing Bill by the arm, unconcerned by the festering feces now oozing between his fingers. "We've found a way. Laxatives can kill them." He held up his water pistol, indicating to Bill that this was the weapon with which he intended to eradicate these beasts.

Bill grinned, his white teeth stained brown. "You don't understand. There's… millions of them down there! They're like… like a… a swarm of bees. It's like a… a… a hive!"

"Wait," said Emily, drawing everybody's attention. "If it really is like a hive, then that must mean there's a queen, right? If we can kill the queen, we can, at the very least, stop any more of these things from being… erm… born."

"And where would we find this 'queen'?" asked David.

"Right here," said Martin, looking back to the sewerage plant. It all made sense now. All the blockages, the sewerage backing up, it was because of some problem here. It had to be. And now they understood what that problem was. It was these things. Their nest was inside the sewerage plant. If they were going to find this queen anywhere, it was here. This was where their final battle was going to take place.

"When all my men had died," said Bill, his eyes wide, his voice now solidified. "I crawled through the sewers, making my way here, thinking that I might be able to warn those in charge, to get them to shut everything down. But I couldn't get in – there were thousands of those fuckers blocking my path. I had to get out of there."

"Well that all but confirms it," said Martin, addressing the entire group. "If there really are that many here, then they must be protecting their queen."

A silence filtered amongst them then. Nobody seemed entirely sure of how they ought to proceed.

Bill was the first to speak up. "Are you sure that laxatives can kill them?"

Martin nodded.

"Okay. Here's the plan – me and you" – he pointed to Martin – "are going in there. We need to find the queen. While we're doing that, you two" – he pointed to David and Emily – "need to go and fetch something for me. Do you think you can do that?"

"What is it?" asked Emily.

CHAPTER SIXTEEN
Descent Into Madness

Martin clicked on the light mounted on his forehead. He peered down into the pipe that seemed to stretch infinitely downward, trailing off into nothingness. Perhaps those religious zealots were right; perhaps, this really was a gateway to hell. For now though, there was nothing in there – as far as he could tell – for him to be concerned about.

Bill had told him about his struggle to escape the sewers, had told him about how he'd had fought for his life with every scrap of energy he had. He'd told him that heading back into the plant in the same way he'd escaped would be an impossibility. As such, they'd needed to find an alternative way in. The entrance they had settled on was via a ladder that extended downward, into the darkness beneath their feet, its point of origin being at the top of a large cooling tower, at least two hundred feet in diameter, and with what must've been a similar height. It had taken more than a few minutes to climb *up* the ladder, which led to the walkway that encircled the perimeter of the cooling tower, and now, as he stared *down* the ladder inside the maintenance access point, he knew the downward climb would take even longer.

"No safety harnesses, I'm afraid," said Bill, nodding towards the attachment point, onto which the maintenance workers would normally hook their lanyard. "If you fall, there's only one way you're going."

"Fantastic," said Martin, hoping that his sarcasm was layered thick enough.

He and Bill were both armed with the Super Soakers now. David had offered his to Bill as he was no longer going to need it. Martin had insisted that they take one of the water pistols with them, just in case they ran into any of those monsters on their way. David and Emily had then driven away from the plant, in the car.

Martin looked to Bill. "Do you want to go, or…" He allowed the sentence to linger, waiting for Bill to finish it off for him.

"Ladies first," smirked Bill.

"Thanks." Martin didn't argue. He swung his leg around the ladder and felt for the nearest rung with his foot. Finding a secure footing, he lowered his other leg and made his way around onto the front of the ladder.

"Don't look down," said Bill, almost ready to laugh. It was as if this were a game to him. But then, he had just watched his men be torn to pieces by these things; perhaps he didn't quite believe any of this was real. Martin was having a hard time believing it himself.

"Thanks for the advice," said Martin. "I'll try not to." He then began to make his way down the ladder, one slow and cautious step at a time. After he'd climbed a couple of meters, a clanging from above told him that Bill had now made his way onto the ladder also. Martin looked up, just to confirm that he was indeed correct, and that Bill was following him, having not decided to run in the opposite direction.

Truth be told, Martin wouldn't have blamed him if he *had* decided to flee.

Despite the advice given to him, Martin had no choice but to look down; the pipe was so dark that it was almost impossible to see where his feet were even going. He could feel for most steps, of course, taking his time so that the arch of his foot settled directly over each rung, perfectly balanced. But still, he occasionally needed to look, to use the light form his headtorch, just to be sure his feet were at least headed in the right direction. The last thing he wanted was to miss a rung and end up tumbling to his death, only to have his corpse devoured by those creatures.

That priest had called them 'demons'. Perhaps that name was apt.

"You okay down there?" Bill called from above, his voice echoing, bouncing from the curved walls a thousand times over.

"I'm just about surviving," said Martin, trying to make light of the situation. His fingers were beginning to ache, the muscles in the backs of his hand beginning to throb, his ligaments begging for mercy. "How about yourself?"

"Never better."

After what felt like an eternity of climbing, Martin imagined they were still only halfway down the pipe. Looking up, the entrance to the pipe was now no more than a pinprick of light. Below, nothing but darkness.

Feces Of Death

There were noises now, that Martin didn't seem to recognise. For a moment he thought that perhaps it was his own breathing, but he slowed himself down, pausing momentarily to listen to his own lungs, and found them to be entirely regular. The breathing of his companion then, perhaps. But, no. These noises were coming from below.

At least, he *thought* they were coming from below. The echo of the pipe meant that the sound seemed to be clouding all around him, hitting his eardrums from all directions. The sound was scattering and slimy, like birds coated in oil. "You hear that?" he called up to Bill.

"Hear what?" Bill replied.

Martin listened harder. Then something caught his eye, movement in the beam of his headtorch.

There was something crawling up the wall.

It looked like a slug, but five times bigger than the variety Martin was used to seeing in his garden. It was long and fat, a wet sheen covering the entirety of its brown body.

And then Martin realised what it was; it was a turd. It was literally a turd, like any other turd, except this one was moving, its body pulsating, stretching and compressing as it slithered up the pipe.

There were more of them too. Hundreds, in fact, all slithering along the pipe, making their way out of the processing plant, and out into the world. Would these things grow even bigger? Would they mutate into something more ferocious, more akin to the creatures Martin had already seen?

He seriously hoped not.

"What the fuck?" muttered Bill, no doubt having finally caught a glimpse of the slugs of shit that were crawling past him.

"Ignore them," said Martin. "I don't think they're dangerous. Come on - we have to keep moving." He hoped he was right. As best he could tell, these things didn't have teeth.

Several minutes later, and Martin spied the corner of the tunnel below, the pipe he was in, and the ladder down which he was climbing, finally coming to an end.

Thank God.

As soon as he was within a safe distance, Martin released his grip of the ladder and dropped to the concrete below. He stretched, cracking his back, bending to rub his hands against his thighs, hoping to wake both up.

Bill dropped from the ladder just a few moments later.

"You okay?" Martin asked.

Bill nodded. "I just hope those things that are climbing out of here don't hurt anyone."

Martin shook his head, emphasising that fact that he didn't believe this would be the case. "They won't," he said. "But we don't need to worry about that right now. We know what we came here to do. It's that which we need to focus on."

Bill nodded his agreement. "Okay then. Lead the way."

***

Emily parked the car a few hundred yards out from where they really needed to be. She could've gotten closer, perhaps, but she figured it wasn't worth the risk. She didn't want them to be seen on their approach. There was no good reason for the two of them to be out there at such a time of night. If anybody saw them, then the entire plan would fall through.

Besides, she didn't like the idea of leaving her car quite so close to the place; she wholly intended on retrieving it tomorrow. Or the day after, perhaps.

The drive had taken them just over twenty minutes, covering the better part of twelve miles. She and David had then walked those final few hundred yards, sticking close to the trees, bathed in their shadows. And now they sat atop a hill, overlooking the PharmaCom factory.

It was exactly as Bill had said it would be. A large building made up the majority of the facility, with several smaller building's dotted around. A series of large chimneys protruded from the top of the main building, a steady stream of white smoke pouring from each. A chain-link fence surrounded the entire property, with the only way in or out being one of the two entry gates – both of which were now closed and locked for the night.

Despite the fact that it was technically out of hours now, the place still seemed to be a hive of activity. People flitted from one building to another, crossing the yard, looking like ants from Emily's current vantage point. The dozen or so floodlights mounted around the yard made the place look as if it existed on some other plane of time entirely, with it being daytime there, but night everywhere else. But that was a silly thought to have. Then again, what *wasn't* silly about all the things that had happened so far today? Not so long ago, Emily had nearly died, killed by a mutant turd, no less. Maybe it wasn't so *silly* to believe that this place actually existed in some parallel universe.

Not that it really mattered.

Within the yard, a number of trucks were parked up. People were loading items onto the trucks, some handballing boxes on, other's carrying barrels in the grip of a forklift. At the end of the line were five trucks that looked different to the others. These ones were chemical tankers, the rear of each consisting of one massive cylinder, laid horizontally, stretching out behind the wagon.

"It's going to be one of those, right?" said David, whispering, despite the fact that they were so far out from the facility there was no chance of them being heard.

And despite this fact, Emily kept her own voice low. "I guess so," she said. "Come on."

They scooted down the hill, keeping low, moving slowly. Emily felt as if she were on some secret military mission, sneaking into the enemy base, ready to take them out, assassinating them one man at a time. She half expected spotlights to begin scanning the surrounding areas, looking for encroaching enemies. And then her brains would be blown out by the sniper in the watchtower. Of course, there were no snipers, and there were no watchtowers. This was just a factory; one, albeit, that was seemingly up to some fucked-up shit.

David and Emily had come prepared. David retrieved a pair of bolt cutters from his bag and began to snip away at the fence, hiding themselves behind the trucks, just hoping that nobody would wander down there, on some random inspection patrol or something. Soon enough, he had formed an opening big enough for the two of them to squeeze through.

Emily had questioned whether all of this was worth it? Couldn't they just ask for the stuff? Wouldn't PharmaCom do whatever it took to clean up their mess? Apparently not. Bill had insisted that PharmaCom – like most billion-dollar corporations – were greedy; they wouldn't be willing to lose that stock, not just for the sake of saving a few thousand lives.

They pushed through the fence, into the compound. Quickly, still keeping their bodies as low as possible (Emily's legs were already starting to burn, the build-up of lactic acid entirely unforgiving), they scurried across the yard, to the chemical tankers.

There were people close by, all men. Emily could hear them talking, laughing, chatting aimlessly about whatever TV show it was that they'd watched last night. She tried to ignore them, moving with as much silent precision as a ninja, praying to God (despite not believing in Him) that nobody would see her.

The back of each tanker was home to a warning sign. It was supposed to tell anybody who looked just what was being transported in the tanker, and what hazards it might pose, should it ever become spilled. They moved along the row of tankers, reading each sign. "Here," said David. "It's this one."

Emily read the sign at which he was currently looking. He was right; this tanker was filled with the same liquid laxative they had filled their Super Soakers with earlier that evening.

The plan was to steal this tanker, drive it to wherever the queen shit was, and dump it into the sewers, killing off these creatures for good.

Emily and David made their way along the side of the tanker. At the front, David reached up and tried the driver's side door.

It was open – why wouldn't it be?

Quietly, he pulled the door open, then helped to boost Emily up. Emily scooted across to the passenger seat, so that David could follow her in. With them both now inside the cab, David closed the door just as quietly as he had opened it. Emily's eyes found their way to the ignition.

The keys weren't there – why would they be?

David slid himself down into the footwell, underneath the steering wheel.

"What are you doing?" muttered Emily, unsure as to whether it was even possible for the men outside to hear her with the doors closed.

"There's no keys," said David, stating the obvious. "I need to hotwire it."

"How do you even know how to do that?"

"Martin taught me. I'm guessing he hasn't told you about that."

Emily was frowning, more annoyed now than she really ought to be. There were still far more important things to be worrying about. "No. He hasn't."

David pulled away a plastic panel from under the dashboard. He then began to pull at the wires inside, dragging them out of the housing. "Yeah, well - back in high school, we used to steal cars, just for the fun of it. We were just kids. It's not somethin' that either of us is proud out. It's just… It is what it is, you know?"

Emily understood – people did dumb shit when they were kids.

The engine of the tanker roared to life, the thunderous sound booming through the cabin. Her eyes wide, Emily quickly sat up.

"You ready for this?" said David, gripping the wheel.

The men outside were looking now, all of them apparently confused as to who it was that had started the tanker, and just where they imagined they might be going. Emily nodded her head.

"Good." David shifted into gear and pressed his foot into the accelerator. The tanker lurched forward, clearly a much bigger, heavier vehicle than anything he'd ever driven before. Emily grabbed onto the handle above her head with one hand, the other hand clasped tightly onto her seat.

Outside, the men ran, diving aside as the tanker ploughed across the yard. David took aim at the gate and floored it. The gate was no match for the mass of the tanker, easily giving way under the vehicle's massive weight.

And then they were gone, out onto the open road, speeding back towards town.

CHAPTER SEVENTEEN
The Nest

An eerie silence filled the sewer tunnels. It was too quiet for Martin's liking. He had expected there to be something more. Quite what, he didn't know. But there should've been *something*. Aside from those slug-like shits, they hadn't seen any other signs of life since entering the tunnels. Bill had insisted there had been an innumerable number of those monsters down here. If that was the case, then where were they?

"Are you sure we're heading in the right direction?" said Martin, not bothering to look back to Bill, who was trailing some distance behind.

"Not *sure*, no," said Bill. "But I *think* this is right." He was carrying a torch in his left hand, the barrel of his Super Soaker rested across his forearm.

Was that a good enough answer? Martin didn't think that it was. Lives were at stake here; they needed to be *certain* about what they were doing. But then, who was Martin to question Bill's direction? He himself didn't know if this was right. They were both just as useless as each other right now, like the blind leading the blind.

Feces Of Death

Martin continued to creep forward, through the darkness, through the silence.

And then his phone rang, a loud jingle echoing through the tunnels.

Martin pulled the phone from his pocket quickly, not wanting to draw any unwanted attention. It was Emily. He answered the call. "Emily?" he said. "Are you okay?"

"We're fine," Emily replied. "We've got the stuff."

Martin was surprised to hear this. He hadn't been so keen on this plan. He hadn't wanted to send Emily off, to break into the facility where these Godforsaken things had been made. Anything could've happened to her. Who knew what might've happened had they been caught. Prison, almost certainly. But would it really have been beyond these people to kill any trespassers? Martin wasn't so sure, and Bill hadn't offered any real reassurance.

But Emily had insisted. She'd seemed almost happy with the plan.

Thankfully, everything had gone to plan – so far.

"Where are you now?" Martin asked.

"Were on our way back to the processing plant," Emily confirmed. "We should be there in around fifteen minutes or so."

"Okay, great."

"Have you found anything yet? We need to know exactly where to dump this stuff, remember?"

"I know. But we haven't found anything yet. As soon as we do, I'll let you know."

"Okay. Well, stay in touch, alright? I love you."
"I love you too."

Martin ended the call then. He was just pleased to hear that Emily was safe. Now he just needed to make sure that he and Bill got out of these sewers in one piece.

"They got the laxative?" Bill asked.

Martin nodded. "They did. They're on their way back here right now."

Bill raised his eyebrows. "We best keep movin' then, huh?"

Martin and Bill continued to follow the tunnels. On more than one occasion, the tunnel split off in different directions, offering them two or three paths they could choose to take. On the first few occasions, Martin had asked Bill for his opinion on which way they should go. Bill always told him to choose, and so Martin had now given up on even asking. The next junction they came to Martin took the left path.

They were right under the plant now, they had to be. But these sewers all looked the same. They looked like any other sewer tunnel, a river of torrid water flowing through, the surface encrusted with all manner of filth and grime. "We should've seen something by now," said Martin, his frustration growing. He turned to face Bill, who instinctively squinted against the light of Martin's headtorch. "You said there were *millions* of them. So, where the hell are they?"

Bill shook his head. "I don't know," he said. "Perhaps they've moved on. Perhaps they found a way out of here, and on to the next town."

"No," said Martin. "That's not what bees would do. If these things really are acting like a swarm – if they *do* have a queen – then they wouldn't move anywhere. They would make their nest, and then do everything in their power to protect it." Only then did it occur to Martin that perhaps they were wrong. Perhaps there was no queen. He'd gotten fixated on this idea, believing it to be true. But the truth was that he had no idea what these things were thinking – if they were even thinking at all. It seemed more likely that they were simply working off instinct. What kind of instincts would a creature born from a puddle of reanimated excrement even have?

"Wait," said Bill. He stared up at the roof of the tunnel, his flashlight dancing across the slimy surface. "When me and my men were attacked, those things were in the water, yes, but they also came from above."

"Right?"

"Well… What's above us right now?"

Martin looked up, only to see exactly what he knew would be there; the solid concrete roof of the tunnel. But what was above there? It wasn't as if it was ground level right above them. There had to be *something* separating them from the road above. The ladder they had climbed down had seemed to stretch on infinitely; they had to be at least fifty meters under the processing plant right now. Martin knew that the plant would stretch someway underground, but they were yet to see any signs.

Were they *under* the processing plant itself?

Martin scanned his surroundings. A ladder to his right trailed up into another pipe. He looked to Bill, hoping to telepathically communicate his thoughts. Bill seemed to understand, his eyebrows raised affirmatively. Martin began to scale the ladder. A few meters above his head, a solid iron cover blocked his path. Hooking his left arm around the rung of the ladder, he pushed the cover with his right hand. It was heavy, his muscles straining against the weight. But then is lifted, squealing as it slid across the floor above.

As soon as the cover was lifted, a vile stench poured through the opening, thickening the air, so much so that Martin would swear he could taste it on his tongue. It was enough to make him gag. For a moment, he considered the fact that it might've been enough to knock him unconscious. He closed his eyes and tried desperately to stifle the vomit wanting to rise from his stomach.

"Fuck me," said Bill, his hand pressed over his nose. "What the fuck is that smell?"

Martin took a deep breath. "It's shit," he said. "I think we're heading in the right direction now."

"Are we going up?"

"I guess so."

Martin continued up the ladder, through the opening, into the tunnel above.

The concrete floor here was layered with excrement. The water flowing through the tunnel was thick and sludgy, like black treacle oozing along in a wide river. The walls were plastered with filth, the same shit dripping from the ceiling in thick globules.

"Oh my God," said Bill, as his head emerged through the hole beneath Martin's feet. "This is fucking disgusting."

Martin reached down and took Bill's hand, helping him up out of the manhole. "Yeah," he said, speaking quietly, his throat dry. "I think we need to be more careful from here on out. We must be getting close."

Bill nodded his agreeance.

Martin's feet squelched through the fecal matter beneath his feet, the gooey substance sucking his shoes in all the way past the soles, then refusing to release him. It was like he was trudging through a field of sodden mud. Except, with every arduous step he took, a hideous odour would be released from the filth, blasting him in the face like a shotgun.

There was noise from somewhere in front. Martin paused, allowing himself to listen over the grotesque sound of his footsteps. Bill paused beside him, his head tipped to one side, listening too. The noise was no more than a dull, monotonous groan, trailing on endlessly. It wasn't the creatures; it was something else. It reminded Martin of an engine trying to turn over, but failing to do so.

Of course – it was the water processing machinery. They were close now; they *had* to be.

Martin's phone began to ring, the high-pitched chirping causing his heart to somersault in his chest. Quickly, he dragged the phone from his pocket.

But it was already too late.

A loud, guttural roar echoed through the tunnel, the sound bouncing from the walls making it impossible to pinpoint its source.

"Oh, fuck!" Bill grunted.

Martin gritted his teeth and lifted his Super Soaker. The light of his headtorch flicked around the tunnel, searching for movement.

Nothing.
No.
Something.
Everything.
Everywhere.

All around.

The shits emerged from the darkness, slithering along the walls and the roof, swimming through the water. Their bodies twisted and compressed, expanding and contracting as they dragged their malleable forms along. Tentacles stretched out from their bodies, wrapping around pipes, their claws digging into the concrete. Some of them had mouths, full to the brim of razor-sharp teeth. Some even seemed to have more than one mouth, positioned diagonally along their bodies like misplaced zippers. Martin's light reflected from the eyes of those that seemed to have them. Those that didn't have eyes didn't appear to be blind; they still approached rapidly, perhaps driven on by some psychic sixth sense.

Martin took aim. He pumped his Super Soaker, then pulled the trigger.

A stream of liquid burst from the nozzle of the gun, spraying over the encroaching monsters. As the liquid hit the creatures, their bodies began to melt, hissing as they burned away, the stink of immolated feces filling the sewers.

Martin's phone was still ringing.

More of the monsters approached. Martin and Bill stood back-to-back, pumping their Super Soakers, and firing at the creatures lurching towards them. The creatures mewled as the liquid burned through their bodies like acid. They roared, wet and guttural, their teeth bared, wide, misshaped mouths gnashing towards their intended prey.

A clawed tendril wrapped around Martin's neck like a snake, lifting him from the ground. The creature hanging from the roof above him drew him

Feces Of Death

inwards, the tendril protruding like a tongue from its mouth, reeling him in like fisherman would his catch of the day. Martin grabbed onto the tendril and tried to pull himself free. His fingertips dug through the soft feces, his palms slipping away uselessly. He could feel the blood leaking from the puncture wounds inflicted to his throat.

"No!" yelled Bill, spinning rapidly, firing a jet of laxative onto the creature that was so close to devouring Martin.

The monster hissed, relinquishing its hold on Martin.

Martin dropped to his knees, struggling for breath. There was no time to dwell on what had just happened to him. He snatched up his Super Soaker and began firing once more. "We need to get out of here!" he said to Bill, his throat growing horse. He felt as if he'd swallowed a bag of needles. "We can't hold them back much longer!"

"I know!" shouted Bill over the hideous roars of the dying beasts. "Get moving then!"

Martin gritted his teeth and pushed forward, spraying any of the creatures that got within four feet of him. Bill matched his footsteps, inching backwards so that their bodies remained pressed together, back-to-back, all angles covered.

Ahead, Martin saw light. Somehow, moonlight was entering this underground cavern. The tunnel ended there, opening out into… God only knew what. But this was their only option. They had no choice but to push through and head on out there, face whatever might be waiting for them.

Bill screamed.

Martin felt Bill's body shift away from his own. He spun. One of the creatures – or perhaps there were two; it was impossible to tell – had wrapped their spiny tentacles around his legs and had dragged him down to the ground. Bill rolled to his front, his fingers scraping against the concrete, trying desperately to find something to grip on to. "No!" he bellowed. "Let go of me! Get the fuck off me!"

Martin dropped to his knees and grabbed Bill by the wrists. The creatures were crawling up Bill's back now, digging their curved talons into the meat of his back, scraping against his spine. One of the things had already began chewing on his foot, its horrifying maw snapping open and shut like a bear trap, blood gushing from Bill's savaged ankle.

His hands slipping due to the noxious mixture of shit and sweat that slicked his palms, Martin pulled as hard as he could, wrapping his fingers around Bill's wrists so tight he could feel the bones inside grinding against each other.

And then a horrifying tearing sound as skin and muscle began to split, bones snapping and ligaments popping. Blood oozed over Bill's lips. He coughed, a fine crimson mist spattering Martin's face.

Still Martin held on, didn't want to let go, didn't want to admit defeat. But those creatures were still approaching from all sides, with no way for Martin to defend himself. He had to let go. He had to leave Bill to die.

Thankfully – although, Martin thought, this was hardly anything to be thankful for – Bill's body split in two then, his legs dragged away by the two creatures there, fighting then over which of them got the spoils. His intestines spilled from his chest cavity, sloughing down into the filthy water. Another of the creatures was on him then, its teeth sinking into his head, sliding through the bone with ease, as if it were as soft as the flesh that surrounded it.

Martin released his grip then, just as Bill's head was bisected, his brain leaking out of his skull.

Quickly, Martin stood. He sprayed those monsters in his immediate vicinity, then ducked his head and ran.

As he exited the tunnel, the ground suddenly disappeared from beneath his feet. The back of his head crashed painfully into the concrete ramp he was now sliding down. He hadn't expected this at all, but he was now in what seemed to be a large funnel, sewerage from two-dozen pipes all filtering into the same place, somewhere deep below, through the black hole into which Martin was himself about to disappear. Above, a large circular grill, the same diameter as the funnel, opened out to the night sky. Martin pushed his heels down, tried to slow his descent. But it was to no avail; the angle was too steep. Although he was still not in the water directly, enough had splashed onto the smooth concrete to make gripping it all of an impossibility.

Martin held his breath as his dropped from the edge of the ramp. He felt sure he was about to fall to his death.

But the drop was over in seconds. His legs crumpled painfully beneath him as his slammed into the steel walkway that crossed the chamber in which he now found himself.

The impact had compressed his lungs, knocking all the air out of his body. Martin closed his eyes, screwed his body into a ball and tried to breathe.

He sucked the air in, his diaphragm aching something fierce. But then something filtered up his nose, something somewhat unexpected; a melodious stench, worse than anything he'd ever smelled before. There was a sound too – a rumble or a gurgle, like an empty stomach trying to digest itself – that seemed to reverberate around the entire room.

Slowly, Martin opened his eyes and pushed himself back, onto his heels. He looked up at the thing towering over him.

This chamber must've been one-hundred-and-fifty feet wide by a hundred feet deep. Above him, the entire ceiling was smothered by an immense creature, its body a vast mass of excrement, pulsating and squirming, shimmering in the minimal light. Legs as thick as tree trunks stretched outward and down the walls. A million tentacles writhed from its undercarriage, like an inverted pit of snakes. There must've been at least a hundred mouths, all strewn across the amorphous form, each one working independently, opening and closing to expose razor teeth. Innumerable eyes littered the exterior of this being, some black, some red, some yellow, all of varying sizes and shapes. In the middle of its body was one large eye; a human-looking organ, the white criss-crossed with bright red veins.

This was the queen.

And she was looking at him.

One of the mouths began to roar. Another joined in then. Than another, and another, and another, until all the mouths had moulded into a chorus of deafening rasps.

Martin clamped his hands over his ears, for fear that the sound might tear through his eardrums. A thick mist filled the chamber; the sickening stench of the monster's breath, expelled from deep within its formless mass. Martin closed his eyes and held his breath, not wanting to inhale this noxious fog.

When the creature stopped roaring, the mist quickly dispersed, allowing Martin to hurriedly scramble up to his feet. He leaned against the railing of the walkway and looked up at the queen. Those tentacles that hung from its undercarriage seemed to shudder, parts shearing off and dropping into the bottom of the chamber. Martin looked down to see these tentacles splattering on the shit-soaked floor below. And then, where they splattered, they began to reform, the expelled excrement sucking back in, reshaping into something more akin to the other creatures Martin had seen previously. These were its babies, being born right before Martin's eyes.

There were more of the monsters surrounding him now, crawling out of the funnel above, dripping down in the cascading sewerage. There were several on the walkway with him, inching slowly forward, their tendrils writhing above them, ready to strike.

Martin closed his eyes and waited to die.

But then his phone was ringing.

Of course! He couldn't die! He still had work to do! He couldn't let any more of these things escape this place, not if there was even the slightest chance of him stopping it. He pulled his phone from his pocket and answered it.

"Oh my God, Martin!" shrieked Emily. "Where are you?"

Martin ignored her question. "Where are *you*?" he asked instead, a far more pressing question.

"We're here. We're at the plant. I tried to call you before, but you didn't answer. I thought you were dead, Martin!"

"I'm not dead," said Martin, *not yet anyway*. "But we don't have much time. I've found the queen. You need to pour the laxative directly into the processor."

"Where?"

"Look for a large grill in the ground. It's an aeration point, to stop the build-up of gasses. Pour it into there."

"Okay. I see it."

Martin closed his eyes as the monsters closed in. He listened as Emily's distant voice instructed David on what he should do – "that's it... over here.... back it up... you need to get closer... come on... hurry..."

"Emily," said Martin, unsure if she could even hear him now. A shitty tentacle wrapped around his neck, claws digging further into the multitude of lacerations that had already been inflicted there previously. "Listen. I need you to know just how much I love you. Okay? I love you more than anything."

"What's that?" said Emily, only just coming back to him. "Martin? What did you say?"

"I said '*I love you*'."

"I love you too."

The creature squeezed, constricting Martin's neck, cutting off the oxygen supply to his brain. Everything went black.

Then...

WHOOSH!

A sudden rush as torrents of water flooded the chamber.

No, not water – liquid laxative.

The translucent yellow liquid smashed into Martin like a tidal wave, knocking him off his feet. The tentacle wrapped around his neck pulled free, the creature dissolving instantly. Martin kicked his legs, righted himself in the fluid, made his way up to the surface. The shit queen was roaring again now, but at a much higher pitch. It sounded as if it were in pain. Large chunks of its body sloughed away from the ceiling. Its massive legs gave out from under it. Huge swathes of excrement peeled from the roof and into the laxative-sewerage mix, crumbling as they were washed away.

Martin held his breath as the current pulled him under. Sharp claws and even sharper teeth tried to slice into his body, but they were too soft, too weak to do so, disintegrating as they made contact. The shitty liquid thrashed Martin around, sucking him down then forcing him up.

He breached the surface once more, to suck in one last lungful of air. He looked up at the queen just in time to see that one massive eye rupture, swelling like a balloon until it popped, black ocular fluid leaking out like a waterfall.

Martin held his breath and ducked back under, allowing the current to take him wherever it wanted to go.

CHAPTER EIGHTEEN
Done With This Shit

Martin had been washed out of one of the pipes just a stones-throw away from the processing plant. It had taken him a minute to regain his senses. For that moment, he laid there, staring up at the sky, allowing his lungs the enjoy all the fresh air they craved. Filthy water swirled around him, a disgusting mixture of piss and shit, the same disgusting excrement clinging to his body. But Martin didn't care. He was alive, that was all that mattered.

No. That wasn't *all* that mattered. Equally important – no, far *more* important – was the fact that Emily was alive too.

But where was she?

Martin climbed to his feet. His body ached. Blood still oozed from the wounds in his neck, but, as he was still alive, so he assumed that none of those cuts had caught any major arteries. At least he had that to be thankful for. He'd still need to pay his doctor a visit tomorrow for some kind of shot; the last thing he wanted was to die of sepsis, not after everything he'd just been through.

Feces Of Death

Feeling as if he were barely alive, or as if he might just fall asleep at any second, Martin lurched like a zombie across the field that separated him from the processing plant. There, just beyond the fence, was the circular grid through which the laxative had been poured. The tanker had been driven through the fence, the posts having been torn from the ground. And there, beside the tanker, was Emily. She was hugged tight into David's shoulder, her chest rising and falling as she sobbed. David's head was tipped back, his eyes closed. He stroked Emily's hair softly, comforting her.

"I'm gone for a couple hours," said Martin, hoping that the mock tone of his voice wouldn't be lost on either of them. "And you're already hitting on my girlfriend?"

Emily pushed away from David. The look on her face told Martin that she wasn't sure if she'd just imagined hearing his voice. But then she saw him. Her face dropped, her eyes wide like those of an abandoned kitten. "Martin?" she bawled. "Is it really you? I thought you were dead!"

"You should be so lucky." Martin smiled the kindest smile he could manage.

Emily ran to him. She wrapped her arms around his neck and jumped, hooking her legs around his waist. She was kissing him then, long and deep, sliding her tongue into his mouth. She showed little concern about the masses of shit now smudged across her face. Martin didn't care either; he was just happy to have her back in his arms.

It didn't taste great though.

When Emily finally pulled away and lowered herself back down to the ground, David offered an extended hand, which Martin promptly shook. "How was it down there?" David asked.

"Fucking disgusting," replied Martin.

"Are they dead?"

Martin nodded. "I think so. We killed the queen. I don't think they'll be coming back any time soon."

"Good," said David. "Because I think it's fair to say that you look like you've been through shit!"

Martin couldn't help but laugh.

Emily, on the other hand, was frowning. "Seriously?" she said. "You're making jokes *now*? Martin could've died!"

David smirked. "What? I'm just saying he looks a bit *flushed* is all!"

Martin could barely contain himself anymore. It was true what they said; sometimes, if you didn't laugh, you'd cry.

As if his laughter were infectious, Emily began laughing too. "What are you laughing at?" she said, as if she didn't realise that she too was now laughing. "It's not funny – not even in the slightest!"

"I don't think I can take any more of this," said Martin, still laughing. He draped his arm around Emily's shoulders and kissed her on the cheek. "Seriously. I'm done with this shit."

***

The clean-up operation took several days. Bodies littered the streets. Blood flowed in rivers along the roads. Well… Perhaps that's a bit of an exaggeration. But, in the end, it was found that more than three hundred people had died that night, slaughtered by those demented creatures that crawled up out of the sewers. Many people were found dead in their bathrooms, where most of the things had emerged. Corpses laid in bathtubs, as if they were bathing in blood. One man was found having been pulled into his toilet, his bones ground to dust, so that he could be dragged into the pipes. Only his head and one of his arms remained, wedged into the toilet bowl, slathered with gore. The had monsters killed indiscriminately – no man, woman or child was safe. There were even reports of babies having been killed. Dogs and cats too. Still, nobody really knew what these things had wanted. Were they simply trying to feed? Just trying to survive? It was clear that they were consuming their victims, but nobody knew if these things even had any kind of a digestive system. Nobody knew if they even needed sustenance of any kind. In the end, the conclusion drawn was that they were simply acting on their basic instincts, their primordial brains driving them to kill and to eat.

A few of the creatures – those not in the sewers when the laxative had been flushed through – had survived. They were quickly eradicated however, by people armed with Super Soakers. Those slug-like shits were even easier to take out, as they moved so slowly.

The entire world heard about the incident. It was all over the news, all over social media. People shared footage of their experiences. Grainy iPhone footage showed the monsters emerging from toilets and from drains, oozing out of kitchen faucets. Videos of people being eviscerated by the creatures, begging for help, their bloodied corpses dragged into the sewers, sprang up all across the internet. Journalists flocked to the scene in droves, each of them hoping to get their very own exclusive from the town that had been besieged by these hideous abominations.

PharmaCom had tried to cover up the incident, but there was little they could do to prevent the massive breach of data that came in the ensuing days. The company was shut down temporarily, as a thorough investigation was carried out. Despite the organization's insistence that they had done nothing wrong, still consumer trust in the brand declined rapidly. This decline in sales, along with the closure of all global operations, cost the company billions. PharmaCom managed to survive however, their military contracts being worth far more than the pharmaceutical division.

Lorry loads of bottled water were delivered into town, so that the water supply could be cut off, the sewers entirely flushed.

And then, after all the funerals and the protests and the investigations, after all the journalists had left town, life just kind-of went back to normal. The whole incident was soon forgotten. The world soon moved on from the fact that a horde of man-made creatures – made living feces, no less – had decimated the population of a town. The world found some other tragedy to fixate on.

But those who lived through the experience never forgot. They just had to get on with their lives as best as possible.

Martin and Emily were married the following year. David was their best man.

And the sewers were silent once again.

Except for the rats of course. They were still down there, reclaiming their home, wallowing in the filth. They crawled along the pipes and swam in the fetid water, feasting on whatever crap got flushed into their lair.

In turn then, the rats themselves became food for those monsters that survived, their withered bodies pulsating as they slithered through the tunnels, waiting for their chance to rise once more.

THE END

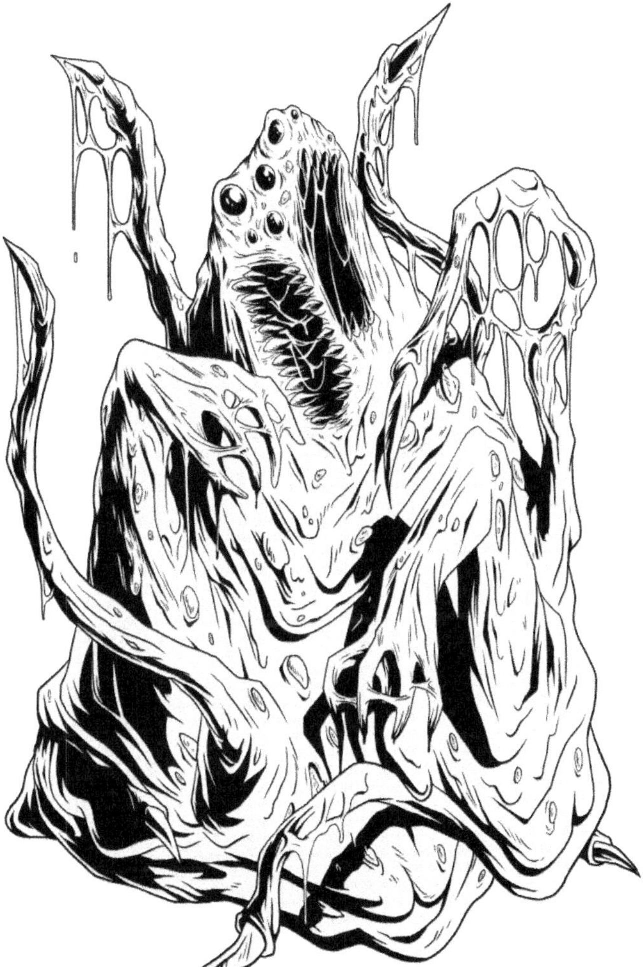

ALSO AVAILABLE

The Whores Of Satan
Bloodhounds
Superfan
Idle Hands
In The Valley Of The Cannibals
Nazi Gut Munchers
The House Of Rotting Flesh
In The Name Of The Devil
Shotgun Nun
Return To The Valley Of The Cannibals
The House Of Rotting Flesh: Episode 2
Teddy Bears Picnic
Night Of The Freaks
Shotgun Nun Vol.2: The Wrath Of God
Feces Of Death

ALSO AVAILBLE FROM
D&T PUBLISHING

Field Trip